HENRY
and the
CHALK DRAGON

HENRY
and the
CHALK DRAGON

by Jennifer Trafton

Illustrations by Benjamin Schipper

RABBIT ROOM
— PRESS —

To Pete,
who loved my imagination
and opened the door

Chapter 1

The Bedroom Door

HENRY PENWHISTLE'S BEDROOM door was the sort of door where adventures began. His mother had painted it with a special kind of black paint that he could draw on with chalk, and when Henry went into his room and closed the door, six feet of black space towered above him like a blank sheet of paper. He drew many loopy, dizzy, spiky, wonderful shapes on the door, and then erased them, and then drew again, and erased again, and drew and erased and drew and erased some more.

Over the years, the black paint began to wear thin and crack. The eraser no longer erased the door completely, and the black space was like a night full of shooting stars—chalky specks of red and orange and yellow and green and blue and purple. Sometimes Henry ran out of chalk and used crayons or markers or pencils or even finger paint instead, and no amount of erasing or scrubbing could get rid of all *those* marks. The drawings floated on the blackness like colorful ghosts.

And one day, on top of all the ghostly shapes and squiggles and smears, Henry drew a picture of a dragon.

It was a Work of Art. The dragon's teeth were like silver daggers. Its wings were so wingish they could have lifted Henry's whole bedroom into the air and carried it to a secret lair on the other side of the sea. Its body was green—*jungle green*, which was Henry's favorite color, because it made him think of exotic creatures and perilous places. This dragon was everything a dragon should be: fierce and fearsome and full of fire.

Henry tossed aside his chalk, stood back to look at the door, and sighed in perfect contentment. He was wearing his raincoat with the aluminum foil taped all over it that glittered like a knight's suit of armor—strong, heroic, invincible armor. He liked the word *invincible*. Nothing could get through his suit of armor. The raincoat came all the way down to his knees, and it had a wide collar and rolled-up sleeves. A silver-duct-tape-covered milk carton with its bottom cut off fit perfectly on his head as a helmet. "I am Sir Henry Penwhistle," he said proudly to the dragon, "and I will slay you!"

Then he dropped to his knees and rummaged under his bed. He drew out a long cardboard tube that had once been in the middle of a roll of wrapping paper covered with tiny Santa Clauses—now it was a sword.

Henry brushed off his armor. He held his sword high.

"You have dared to invade the town of Squashbuckle, and I am its protector. Prepare to meet your doom!" Henry jumped over the drawings of dragon-fighting monster trucks that covered the floor. Waving his sword in sweeping circles, he whirled past the overflowing book chest with its stirred-up soup of favorite stories—stories about wild things and unlikely heroes, chocolate factories and tiny motorcycles, buried giants and mock turtles. "Where did you hide the prisoners?" he yelled. "Show me, or there'll be nothing left of you but chopped dragon liver!"

But the dragon did not move. It was a stubborn beast, and wily as a snake.

"Aha! You're going to be tricky, are you? Well, let's see if you can dodge my super sneaky sideways sword swipe!" Henry climbed onto the bed and took a bouncing leap over his play dough sculptures of trees and towers. He kicked his legs, spun around, sliced the air with his sword, and landed in a pile of dragon poop—which had once been green socks.

"That was awesome," he whispered. "I've got to draw that part." Dropping the cardboard tube, he crawled over to his bed. Then he pulled a book out of a secret place under his mattress that no one knew about but him. It was a sketchbook with blank pages for drawing, and on the cover he had written in tall, grand letters:

SIR HENRY'S QUEST

Quest. It was probably the best word of all the words ever made up. It meant *going on a really long journey to find something you want a whole lot.* Oscar Rockbottom had helped him to spell it right.

Oscar was Henry's best friend.

If life were a drinking straw, Oscar would be the paper wrapper soaring off the end.

But even Oscar had only occasionally been allowed to peek inside the sketchbook.

The book was a record of all of Henry's adventures. It was a story—Henry's very own story, a story made with pictures—and he imagined someone adding words to the pictures someday and making it into a *real* Book, like the books in his book chest. But it would be a secret Book no one else could read. *Sir Henry's* adventure. *Sir Henry's* quest. How would it end? He didn't know, but he knew he would be a great hero and save the entire world.

Looking through the sketchbook was like stepping into his story. On one page, King Kong, the giant gorilla, was beating his hairy chest and carrying off Henry's teacher, Miss Pimpernel. Henry still remembered his mother's face the day he drew that—she had walked into his room just as he was leaping from the bed to the dresser, chasing after the gorilla and pretending to swing on jungle vines like Tarzan. On the next page, Abraham Lincoln was wearing his tall black hat and looking relieved on the day Henry had traveled back in time and saved the Civil War from being invaded by aliens. Across another page raced a pirate ship with Henry himself, sword in hand, battling a peg-legged pirate.

That ship had been his favorite drawing—until now. The dragon, the marvelous chalk dragon, beat them all.

A breeze made the pages flutter, and Henry jumped to his feet and ran to shut the window. Outside, the real night sky with its real shooting stars (not chalky ones) crowded around the Penwhistle house, trying to spy on the knight and his adventure. But Henry pulled the curtains closed. He and the world had a deal: he would keep away from its silly chatter and its honking horns, its math equations and its shopping malls, its confusing rules and its laughing faces. And in return, the world would keep out of his bedroom.

For in *this* room, behind *this* door, lay a deeper magic and a wilder story than the world had ever seen. Or ever *would* see—as long as the door stayed shut.

Henry opened his sketchbook to a blank page, and there he drew the wonderful dragon that was on his door. "Hold still," he told the dragon sternly. He drew the dragon poop and the trees and the towers and dragon-fighting monster trucks, and he drew himself leaping off a mountain and doing the super sneaky sideways sword swipe.

Then he let the pencil drop to the floor and shut the book quickly. He could have sworn the dragon's eyes had turned towards his castle. It was made entirely of Legos, matchsticks, shoelaces, tissues, Scotch tape, and gumdrops. He had spent a whole week building it piece by piece. Henry picked up his sword and dashed to the castle gate. "Oh, no you don't! I will defend Camelot from—"

He stopped. Behind the castle, in the corner of the bedroom, was another pile of Legos. It was the ruins of a scientific laboratory, with a broken Lego microscope and toilet-paper-roll test tubes and a magnifying glass made of plastic wrap stretched over a bubble wand. Oscar had built it.

Oscar was Henry's best friend.

Except for sometimes.

And one of those *sometimes* was still hovering, like a dark cloud of memory, around the little plastic laboratory. Henry shoved it all into the closet and shut the closet door so he wouldn't have to think about it.

"You kidnapped Oscar, didn't you? I knew it. Where are you keeping him?" Henry aimed his sword at the dragon's heart. "What? Of course he's not a *knight*," he scoffed as if the dragon had spoken. "He's a *scientist*. Last summer he was an astronaut and built a spaceship in his garage. And now he's a *paleontologist*. He studies fossils and dinosaurs and things that are really old and dead. He even dug up an ancient birdbath in his backyard. A pterodactyl probably used it. Anyway, he's *important.*"

The dragon stared back at Henry, unblinking and unimpressed.

"So," Henry continued, "I demand that you let him go this instant."

Suddenly the chalk dragon swung toward him, turned around, and beat its head against the wall—because Henry's mother had opened the door and swung it wide.

"*Mom,*" wailed Henry, "you always *interrupt!*"

CHAPTER 2

A LETTER FROM A SUPERVILLAIN

HENRY WHIPPED the sketchbook out of sight as his mother walked into the room and began picking dragon poop off the floor. "It's time to go to bed," Mrs. Penwhistle said, and before Henry could save them, she had scooped up all the socks and put them in the clothes hamper. His mother could clean a house faster than a tornado could carry it away to the Land of Oz. Henry scrambled around the room grabbing drawings and sculptures and pushing them under his bed.

"Can't I see them?" Mrs. Penwhistle asked.

"No!"

His mother's smile had little wings, like a bird.

Sometimes it flitted and danced across her face, sometimes it settled there softly, and sometimes it flew away and hid for hours behind a dresser or inside of a vase of flowers. Henry watched it fly away now, and he was sorry. "Henry!" she said.

"They're not ready to be looked at yet . . . please."

She might see the one with the purple one-eyed monkeys leaping off the moon and think it was scribbling and pat his head as if he were a kindergartner. But it was *not* scribbling. It was Art.

His mother licked a finger and tried to rub out a squiggle of blue in the upper right-hand corner of the door. "Is this a marker spot? You know you can't use marker on this door. It won't erase!"

"Mom, *please* don't! That was a Puffleburpachoo."

"A *what*?"

"You rubbed out its tooth. It has a Very Unusual Tooth."

Mrs. Penwhistle sat down beside him on the edge of the bed and said "Henry" in a tone that he knew all too well. It meant that something not-so-nice was coming, and so she was trying to sound extra nice about it. "Principal Bunk just called." (Henry sighed and slumped deeper into his raincoat-armor.) "And he said that you had a letter for me that I am supposed to sign."

Henry took off his helmet and let it drop to the floor. Principal Bunk was a supervillain, and his dastardly plot to enslave the world had apparently begun with Henry. He fished around in his backpack and handed a crumpled piece of paper to his mother.

Mrs. Penwhistle unfolded the letter, cleared her throat, and began to read.

Dear Mr. and Mrs. Penwhistle,

Warm greetings from La Muncha Elementary School! I regret to tell you that we are concerned about your son Henry. He has refused to participate in this week's class art project. This is surprising, since usually Henry wants to do nothing BUT draw. Last week during a science lesson, for example, his class was supposed to be memorizing a list of tree species native to our region. But instead, Henry drew a tree with tentacles coming out of the branches, covered the trunk with eyes, and colored the grass purple and the sky orange. This is simply not scientifically accurate. Perhaps you could take him to visit a few trees to show him what they look like, or give him a new pair of eyeglasses.

"I don't need glasses," Henry retorted. "I see more than everybody else!"

"Purple grass?" said his mother. Her cheeks were twitching. The smile was inside, beating its wings and trying to come out, but she wouldn't let it. "Tentacles in the trees?"

"Sometimes there are," he mumbled. "Sometimes no one else is paying attention."

Mrs. Penwhistle turned back to the letter.

Henry will surely fail the science test if such shenanigans continue, and I'm concerned that the rest of the class may begin following his lead.

Henry snorted. No one in his class would ever follow his lead! He remembered Simon Snoot's rude laughter when Miss Pimpernel had pointed out the purple grass, and how the others had giggled and whispered.

What if other children start believing that the sky is orange and that trees have tentacles? What would happen to test scores? The reputation of our school is at stake. We teach our students what is TRUE. Arithmetic and shoelaces and presidential elections are true. Giant cloud people, tentacled trees, and fire-breathing dragons are not true.

As his mother read, something happened to the dragon—a ripple happened, like the little waves that wrinkle the water when you drop a pebble into a puddle. The silver-dagger teeth fell open, just slightly, and the golden dragon-eyes turned to glare at the two human beings sitting on the bed. For a brief moment, the dragon didn't look fierce and fearsome and full of fire. The dragon looked *insulted*.

"Did you see that?" Henry gasped.

"What?"

"The dragon moved."

"A breeze from the window just made the door sway a little."

"No, the door didn't move, the *dragon* moved."

"Of course it didn't move, honey. It's only a drawing.

Dragons aren't real. You know that, right?"

Henry peered hard at the door, but the surface was as still as a frozen lake. No rippling at all. *Dragons aren't real. Dragons aren't true.* "Are *real* and *true* the same thing?" he was about to ask, but his mother had picked up the letter again and was reading.

> *Which brings me to this week's art project. It is National Vegetable Week, and we are taking a break from our test preparation to hold an art show tomorrow in the cafeteria. All of the classes are contributing a Work of Art (promoting vegetables, of course) to the art show, where their talents will be greatly admired and applauded by one and all. But twice Henry has been sent to my office because he turned in a blank piece of paper. I trust that your wise parental guidance will convince him to turn over a new leaf (without tentacles). Surely he would like for his artwork to be admired and applauded as well!*
>
> *Your humble public servant,*
> *Principal Cleaver Bunk*

"But Henry," said Mrs. Penwhistle. "You love art! Why wouldn't you participate in the art project?"

"Because..." Henry hung his head low. He was ashamed to say it. Ashamed that Miss Pimpernel, who should have known better, had come up with such a tragically, embarrassingly awful idea. "Because it's a box," he said. But it was worse than that. So much worse. He had to whisper it: "A box of . . . *bunnies.*"

"I see," his mother said, pulling her mouth into a frown to match Henry's. "Bunnies."

"I *hate* bunnies. And we have to trace around a cardboard bunny shape so they'll all look the same, and they're eating *lettuce,* and Miss Pimpernel is gluing them all over a big box to hang from the ceiling."

"And you won't do it?"

"I *can't.*"

"Oh, Henry," his mother said gently. "You didn't even try? I bet your drawing would be the best in the whole class!"

"I *did* try," said Henry. He had stared and stared at the paper. His imagination had been whirling with pictures, and the pictures in his imagination had wiggled down into his arm and kicked inside of his fingers, wanting to come out. But he knew they were the wrong pictures. They were pictures of purple lettuce leaves growing upside-down out of the nostrils of a three-eyed asparagus monster. They were pictures of rabbits that jumped so high they tore holes in the clouds and landed on Mars. His drawings would be different from everyone else's. They would be laughed at. And so he had to shake the pictures out of his fingers and squeeze them back into his imagination and shut the door of his brain tightly so they wouldn't come out. "A hanging box of bunnies is the *worst* Art Project *ever*," he sighed.

For just a second, the corner of his mother's mouth fluttered upward. But then she coughed and was thoughtful again. "Do you know what I think? I think you should take some of your other drawings to school and show your teacher and Principal Bunk. Let everyone see what a good artist you are."

"No! I'm never taking any art to school. Ever again." He thought he saw the dragon frown at him, but he looked away quickly.

"I hope you'll feel differently tomorrow." His mother picked up one of his crayons, signed her name at the bottom of the letter to show she'd read it, and put the letter neatly into his backpack. "Why don't you *practice* drawing bunnies on your bedroom door tomorrow morning before school, just to see if you like it. Then it will be easier to draw one for your class. Bunnies are so cute. And safe. And not quite so many colors." She looked at the door again, and little worry wrinkles crinkled over her eyebrows. "That *is* an awfully scary dragon."

"I'm not scared of it," Henry said, eyeing the door again, but there was no movement.

Henry was telling the truth. Dragons aren't scary—well, they are, but they're a good kind of scary. They're the kind of scary you *want* to be scared of. People are the bad kind of scary, he thought. Dragons can only eat you, but people can laugh at you, and that is like being chewed to death by a smile.

Mrs. Penwhistle sighed and gently took off Henry's armor. He got into bed, and she tucked the covers around him and between his feet the way he liked it. "Can you promise me something?" she said. "Promise me that tomorrow you'll draw a pretty picture of a bunny."

Henry imagined a bunny with laser-beam eyes, leaping

from planet to planet, swishing galaxies aside with its gigantic fireball tail, chewing spaceships as if they were carrots. The Rowdy Red Rabbit of Doom. It had a bouncy rhythm to it, like the beat of an ominous drum.

The Rowdy Red Rabbit of Dooooooooom . . .

The Rowdy Red Rabbit of Dooooooooom . . .

"Okay, I'll draw a bunny," he said.

"And you'll erase the scary dragon?"

In his mind he was already chasing the Rowdy Red Rabbit of Doom down a black hole into Wonderland. "I'll erase it," he said. And then he almost jumped out of his bed, because a poof of chalk dust had exploded silently from the door in an angry *huff* and was filling the room with a jungle- green haze. He blinked, and the dust was gone.

"Good night, Henry. I love you." His mother kissed him on the forehead, and the kiss was like the warm footprint of a new story on his brain.

"Can you close the door please?" he called out as she left the room.

The door swung shut, and the dragon reared its head—fierce and fearsome and safely stuck on the door where it belonged.

Henry pulled a flashlight from underneath his pillow. Every so often he would turn on the flashlight and shine it on the door. The colorful chalk dragon seemed to roar at him. Light off—all was still. Light on—the golden eyes watched him without blinking. Light off—the pictures in his head danced in the dark. Light on—the picture on his door glowed with life. Light on. Light off. Light on. Light off. After about an hour, he fell asleep.

In the very early hours of the morning, Henry had a dream—or he thought it was a dream. He dreamed that something was hovering above him, looking down at him. He dreamed that he felt hot breath on his face. And before his alarm clock even rang, he sat straight up in bed, wide awake. Someone had opened his bedroom door.

He got up and closed the door, and then he saw it. His bedroom door was black—a solid wall of black, like a rectangular hole. There were no smears or smudges or scratches or squiggles. There were no ghostly shapes on it at all. And there was no dragon.

As Henry dressed for school, he kept looking nervously at the door, peering at it from different angles. But there it stood, as black and empty as a starless night.

On the floor by his bed was his invincible suit of armor and his silver helmet. He looked at his armor, then back at the door. This was a morning that needed a knight.

He put the raincoat on over his school clothes and placed the milk carton on his head. Then he reached under the bed for several things that might come in handy on an adventure and stuffed them into his backpack—a cowboy hat and lasso, binoculars, a gorilla mask, a couple of pirate eyepatches. Last of all, he threw in a few pieces of chalk and the eraser. He was ready.

Henry peered underneath the door and down the hallway. He sniffed the door, but not the slightest whiff of chalky-crayony-pencily-painty scent tickled his nose.

"Be brave, Sir Henry," he whispered to himself. "Be brave." He reached out his hand very slowly and turned the doorknob.

It is a dangerous thing to open a door. But that, after all, is the only way to find an adventure.

CHAPTER 3

THE X-TREME TURBO-ROBOTIC NANO-KNUCKLE ANTI-GRAVITY THUNDER-CRUSHER

HENRY RAN DOWNSTAIRS to find his mother and father standing in the living room, scratching their heads and staring at a trail of disaster. "What on *earth*?" Mr. Penwhistle said. A chain of food stretched across the floor—open cans of baked beans, smashed grapes, crumbled potato chips, half-eaten carrots, and cheese-flavored crackers chewed up and spit out in little orange blobs. There were strange tooth marks in the arms of one of the armchairs. *Dragon teeth?* wondered Henry.

An enormous golden retriever bounded into the room barking with excitement. "Oh, Furdinand, look what you've done!" groaned Mr. Penwhistle. "For the last time,

22

you may *not* eat the house!" He knelt and began wiping up cracker blobs with a napkin.

"That—that—that *dog!*" sputtered Mrs. Penwhistle. Furdinand innocently sniffed a piece of hamburger and wagged his tail.

Henry's father turned and saw Henry standing at the foot of the stairs in his suit of armor. "Good morning, Squirt! Too bad you weren't here to protect the castle from our villainous dog!" Henry sighed. He was probably the only knight in the world whose dad called him Squirt. *Sir Squirt.* It sounded like an orange with a drinking straw stuck in it. Wearing a bow tie. "Going out to rescue damsels in distress today? You know—" Mr. Penwhistle winked "—*girls?*"

"I'm going to feed them all to the dragon!" said Henry, whirling his sword around as if he were poking it through frilly pink dresses and piling them up on a dinner plate.

"Henry, where is your chivalry?"

"Inside my armor, where it always is."

"Then you'd better look under your left collar."

Chivalry was all the rules a knight had to live by in order to be a good knight. To keep himself from forgetting the rules, Henry had written in his armor every bit of chivalry he had ever heard of or read about. Sometimes he pulled his hands and his head into his armor like an aluminum-foil-covered turtle, until all he could see were the colorful scribbles of chivalry all around him. Scrawled on the inside of the raincoat were rules like **BE BRAVE** and **FIGHT FOR THE RIGHT** and **EAT YOUR SPINACH** (well, okay, that was for Popeye) and **COUNT YOUR BLESSINGS BEFORE THEY HATCH** (he wasn't sure that one was quite right).

He looked under his left collar, and a blob of bright blue marker said:

DON'T FEED GIRLS TO DRAGONS.

Oh.

"Well, whatever you do," said Mr. Penwhistle, "be careful not to let your imagination run away with you. You don't want to end up like Dennis Duckman, do you?"

"Who's Dennis Duckman?"

"Right fielder on the Squashbuckle Little League team. Always daydreaming. He let his imagination run away with him—picked him up right in the middle of the ninth inning, leaped over the dugout, and carried him away. No one ever saw him again. Imagination. One of the most powerful forces in the universe, you know. Can't be too cautious."

His father winked, and Henry couldn't figure out whether or not he was teasing him.

"Bill, don't put ideas in his head," Mrs. Penwhistle said. She looked at Henry and sighed. "Hurry up and get ready before the bus comes. I hope you're not going to school with the milk carton on your head."

"It's my helmet," Henry reminded her. Her smile was nowhere to be seen. Henry peered around the house, hoping to catch a glimpse of the smile's little wings fluttering at the windowsill, or in the pile of laundry, or on top of the china cabinet.

And that's when he saw it.

Not the smile.

The X-treme Turbo-robotic Nano-knuckle Anti-gravity Thunder-crusher.

His Uncle Frank had given him a toy just like it last Christmas, and after five minutes, Henry had realized that it was just a big, boring hunk of plastic. He had much more fun drawing it on his door than actually playing with it. But this one looked different. It looked like something—something jungle-green—*pretending* to be an X-treme Turbo-robotic

Nano-knuckle Anti-gravity Thunder-crusher. And as Henry watched, it quietly and slowly rolled *up* the stairs.

"I forgot something," Henry said, scrambling up the steps two at a time. Furdinand barked and tried to follow him, but Mr. Penwhistle took the dog firmly by the collar and pulled him toward the door. "Oh, no you don't, Furdinand," he said. "You're going outside."

In the upstairs hallway, a wonderful change was taking place. Just as, last night, the rippling *something* had traveled through the dragon, the toy rippled and shivered. The Anti-gravity parts were tumbling off. The Turbo-robotic parts were going up in smoke. The X-treme parts were exploding into grumpy greenness. The Nano-knuckles became knobbly nostrils. And two thunderous feet stood ready to crush an unlucky passerby to bits.

Henry recognized the curve of those horns and the arrow-tipped tail. He recognized every sharp green flick of scaly skin, every zigzag of the bony spines running down the creature's back. It was his dragon. Just as he had imagined it. Just as he had drawn it. Here it was, standing in front of him! There was something brand new in the world, and he had put it there!

There is a kind of fear that squeezes your heart with an icy hand and freezes you into a popsicle. But there is another kind of fear that is thrilling and hot, that makes your fingers tingle and your toes tickle each other inside your shoes until you want to leap over the Empire State Building. Henry was afraid with this kind of fear, and it felt *good*.

The dragon stared back at him—up and down, from his sneakers to his shiny helmet. It did not look afraid of Henry. It spread its wings proudly. It stretched its scaly neck as high as it would go. Its mouth widened slowly into a dragonish grin.

How long had Henry been waiting for this moment? Here he was, in his shiny suit of armor, with a sword in his hand. And here was a real live dragon—a dragon who could knock the house down with a few flicks of its tail, who could eat his mother for breakfast, who could send a ball of fire bouncing down the street. He knew exactly what he had to do.

He jabbed his sword into the dragon's scaly stomach. "Take that, you beast! I am Sir Henry Penwhistle, and I will slay you!"

The dragon's grin disappeared. Its golden eyes squeezed themselves into thin, glittering slivers. Then it bent over and snatched the cardboard tube in its enormous jaws. Henry watched his beloved sword fly out of his hands and disappear down the dragon's throat.

"Hey!" Henry cried.

The dragon swept past him into the bedroom, its nostrils twitching. Henry heard a mighty *sniff* and suddenly a dozen of his drawings were sucked from under his bed and stuck to the dragon's snout. The dragon pulled them off one by one, licked a monster truck, sniffed a monkey, then opened its mouth and swallowed the pictures whole.

"HEY!" Henry cried more loudly. "That's my Art!"

Art! That gave him an idea. Henry's favorite book since he was four years old was *Harold and the Purple Crayon*. All Harold had to do was draw what he needed, and it was there. So Henry turned to the blank door, picked up a piece of white chalk, and drew a magnificent sword, a knight's sword, a sharp, shiny, dragon-slaying sword—but nothing happened. He opened the door. He closed it. The sword stayed on the door, not moving, not changing, just sitting there looking flat and chalky and wonderful like a drawing is supposed to do.

Henry drew the sword again with a purple crayon. Nothing happened.

He poked his head into the closet and pulled out a silvery feather duster that shimmered and poofed out when he rolled the handle between his hands. Not very knightly, but it would have to do for a sword.

Meanwhile, the dragon had stomped over to the castle in the corner of Henry's room. The dragon's mouth opened wide. Its teeth were like a ring of daggers around the opening of a cave, and the cave was growing larger and larger and larger.

"No!" said Henry. He dropped his backpack and leaped onto the dragon's tail. "Don't eat that! You are not allowed to eat that. You are *my* drawing and you have to do what I say."

Without even a single *crunch*, the castle—flags and all—disappeared down the dragon's throat. The dragon burped.

Henry forgot to be the good kind of afraid and began to be angry. "I worked really hard on that castle!" And with all his strength he jumped and landed on the dragon's foot.

But again the dragon took no notice of Henry. It was staring at something else on the floor—Henry's backpack.

The rippling change began again. Shapes danced across its face—and they were shapes that Henry recognized, because he had drawn them all, first on his door, then in his sketchbook—the golden squiggles of a lion's mane, the loopy lines of a turkey with its wiggly red beard-thing and a Thanksgiving pilgrim's hat on its head, the long orange neck of the Loch Ness Monster (orange because he had run out of green chalk that day) with scratches of blue crayon waves . . .

Finally, one shape settled on its face, and a long green horn sprouted from the dragon's head. Under the horn a wrinkly body burst out, and a rhinoceros charged straight at Henry's backback.

A rhinoceros? The dragon was now a rhinoceros?

The green horn stabbed the backpack and shook it until everything fell out. The rhinoceros stuck its head inside, and then one foot, and then another, and tried with all of its might to squeeze its enormous body into the little bag.

Henry backed away and stuck his hand into the secret place under his mattress. He flipped quickly through his sketchbook until he found the drawing he was looking for—it was a picture of Sir Henry chasing Mr. Preposterous Rhinoceros, so preposterous that it was trying to escape by squeezing itself into a bathtub drain. He flipped the pages to other drawings. An octopus. A spider. A snake. Would the rhinoceros change back into a dragon, or would it change into something else?

Henry didn't have to wonder very long. The rhinoceros turned a deep shade of jungle-green all over and began to shrivel and pucker and shrink. Its four legs each split in half and stretched like wet noodles into eight tentacles. And Henry's poor backpack, instead of being invaded by a rhinoceros, was now being hugged to death by an octopus as it tried to fit all of its tentacles inside.

"Stop that!" Henry said, tossing aside the sketchbook and tugging the backpack away from the octopus. All of the wonderful tingly excitement he had felt when his Work of Art had stood there alive in front of him was now gone. For he knew now that the dragon-rhinoceros-octopus was not interested in having chivalrous battles. This dragon, like most dragons, was a thief. It had stolen all the shapes he had drawn on his door. It was *becoming* them, trying them on like colorful clothes.

And it wanted to go to school.

"Henry?" his mother called. "The bus is coming! Hurry up!"

"Just a minute! I'll be right there! *Don't come upstairs!*"

He grabbed the octopus by the head. It slipped right through his hands like a blob of green jello. He grabbed it again, digging his thumbs in, and lugged it over to the door. Squirming tentacles with little round suckers curled around him as he tried to squish the wiggly shape onto the black space where it had once been safely stuck. "Get back up there on the door where you belong," he whispered.

But it was like squishing the white fluffy explosion of popcorn back into the kernel again. The Art was out, and it would not go back in.

Henry dove for the backpack. Kicking back the tentacles with his feet, he stuffed in the papers and the books and the cowboy hat and rope and all of the other things the rhinoceros had tossed out, and then he put his sketchbook in as well and zipped the pack closed.

The octopus-dragon wiggled and squiggled against the

zipper, but fortunately tentacles are not very good at unzipping things.

"No, you cannot go to school with me!" said Henry.

"Henry, I'm not going to school with you!" called Mrs. Penwhistle. "What is that noise? Are you okay?"

"I'm-okay-nothing's-wrong-please-don't-come-in-my-room!"

The octopus-dragon pounded its tentacles petulantly against Henry's backpack.

"No!" Henry squirmed out of its grasp and ran out of the room. Just before he swung the door closed, a tentacle shot out and latched onto his backpack with one of its suckers. Henry pushed against the door. The tentacle wedged itself in the crack. Henry yanked on the backpack. The tentacle stretched.

"I have—" (push)

"to draw—" (yank)

"BUNNIES!"

The sucker popped off, the tentacle slithered away, and the door slammed shut. Henry sat braced against it, hugging his backpack safely against his chest.

"Henry?"

His parents were standing at the top of the stairs.

Henry's stomach melted into his socks. He pulled himself into his armor like a turtle and looked for some chivalry to help him.

TELL THE TRUTH said a big orange scrawl.

Henry took a deep breath. "There's a dragon in my bedroom! I mean an octopus. I mean, the dragon turned into a rhinoceros and *then* into an octopus . . ." He felt his voice getting smaller and smaller. "*After* it ate all the cheese crackers and pretended to be an X-treme Turbo-robotic Nano-knuckle Anti-gravity Thunder-crusher." A jungle-green spider scuttled underneath the door, pranced down the hallway, and disappeared down the stairs.

In all of the great stories of knights and chivalry that Henry had ever heard, the knights never had to explain to their parents why their bedrooms were suddenly dragon-less, rhinoceros-less, and octopus-less. They never had to ask to stay home from school in order to protect the neighborhood from a fire-breathing spider. And if they *had* asked, they certainly wouldn't have been told that school was more important.

But Sir Henry Penwhistle did not live in one of those

stories. And so he very soon found himself strapping his backpack to his back, grabbing the lunchbox that his mother had set out for him by the front door, and running to catch the bus.

"Bunnies, Henry!" Mrs. Penwhistle called after him. "Bunnies!"

CHAPTER 4

A LUNCHBOX AND A QUEST

THE DOOR OF THE BUS screeched as it folded up to let Henry on and screeched again as it unfolded behind him. The bus driver, Mr. Bruce, laughed and slapped his knee. "Sir Henry, you are the shiniest star in the sky this morning!"

When Henry had been in kindergarten, he would sit in the front seat and listen to Mr. Bruce tell stories all the way to school. His favorite was the one about the boy who pulled a sword out of a stone and then grew up to be King Arthur. But Henry was much more grown up now and would rather be turned into a toad by Merlin than be seen sitting with the kindergartners. He found a seat near the middle of the bus and scrunched up against the window.

"Look at him—he's covered in aluminum foil!" said Simon Snoot.

Simon Snoot was Henry's mortal enemy. If life were a drinking straw, Simon Snoot would be the heel smooshing it flat on the ground. He spent so much time scrunching his face into scornful shapes that it looked like his nose had been smooshed. Henry could never think of him as just Simon. He was always Simon Snoot.

Simon Snoot elbowed the boy next to him, and their laughter bounced from seat to seat to seat.

When Mr. Bruce laughed, it was as if he shared a secret joke with you that no one else would understand. But when the other kids laughed, Henry was the joke. And now, all his noble feelings of knightliness vanished.

"He looks like a leftover pizza," said one boy.

"Is that a *milk carton* on his head?" said another, giggling.

"He's so weird."

The bus bumped and burped as it started moving. Henry slumped lower into his seat.

"Hi, Henry," said Marybeth, smiling over the top of the seat in front of him. "That's a nice shiny outfit. What is it?"

He could answer Marybeth, of course. But there was no telling what might come out of his mouth. He could try to say, "I'm a brave knight, and this is my invincible suit of armor," but instead he might hear himself say, "Goofrashtashbooglegobblegoophead." Henry had learned that words don't always behave themselves around girls.

"Can I try on your shiny hat?" persisted Marybeth.

I'd rather feed you to the dragon, thought Henry. But he remembered his chivalry and began to lift his helmet gently off his head. Before he could give it to her, however, Simon Snoot dropped a cricket down the back of his neck.

"Aaaaaaaaaaaaaaaaaaaaaaaaaaaaaaaah!" squealed Henry, which was the most he had said on the school bus all year. The cricket tried desperately to escape from its strange new raincoat prison, and Henry hoped desperately that it would. Finally it jumped out of his sleeve, crouched on the floor under his seat, and rubbed its legs together in a sad, beautiful song. Laughter echoed around Henry's ears like a kettledrum.

That's what you get for trying to be nice to someone, Henry thought. He sank down into his armor. Armor was supposed to protect you from crickets. A scratchy sentence in black crayon stared back at him from the inside of his raincoat:

DON'T STICK ANYTHING IN YOUR EAR SMALLER THAN YOUR ELBOW.

Sometimes his armor was helpful. Sometimes it wasn't.

He pulled his sketchbook out of his backpack and flipped through the pages slowly. So many drawings had towered over him on his chalky bedroom door as he had played the parts of his story in the little world of his room—until this morning, when the dragon had stolen them all and escaped. Now what was he going to do? He stared out the window at the cars and trees and houses whizzing by. It's hard to go on a quest when a school bus is taking you in the opposite direction.

Suddenly *Sir Henry's Quest* flew out of his hands.

"Whatcha got there, milk brain?" said Simon Snoot, holding the sketchbook away from Henry's grasp and opening it, as a dozen other kids scrambled around him.

"Whoa," said Simon, stretching the book wide with his greasy fingers.

"What *is* that thing?" the boy beside him sneered.

It's the World's Slimiest Giant Slug, thought Henry, but he didn't say it, because one of them might answer: "That doesn't look like a slug at all! It looks like a fat cucumber!" Or even worse: "No wonder! It looks just like *you*!"

Instead he tried to yell, "Give it back!" in a knightly sort of voice (though it came out more like a mouse's squeak) and climbed over the seat to save his book. The boys surrounding Simon Snoot laughed, and Henry tumbled to the floor, holding on tightly to his helmet and swinging his feather-duster-sword.

The bus screeched to a halt. Henry could hear Mr. Bruce's huge footsteps coming down the aisle. The boys scurried back to their places.

"Simon Snoot! It would be a tragic thing, indeed, for a boy to grow up to be a villain. Think of it . . . with your intelligence you could be a president or an astronaut or a world-famous circus entertainer! Don't sully the honor of your good name by being a bully and a book-stealer." He took the sketchbook away from Simon, who was looking red in the cheeks, and flipped through it. "These are good!" Mr. Bruce bellowed. "Henry, you're a talented artist. You shouldn't keep that talent hidden away in a little book. You should let it out!" He handed the sketchbook back to Henry, who held it protectively. "The big art show is today, isn't it? Hoping to come by the cafeteria myself to take a look at all the artsy vegetable things you kids have been working on. You tell that lovely Lunch Lady of yours that Mr. Bruce wouldn't miss it! Now that's a damsel with a good noggin on her neck." Then he gave a final look of warning to the other boys and walked back to the front of the bus.

Part of Henry wanted to die of embarrassment right there on the spot, and part of him felt happiness swell up in his chest like a bubble.

"Henry, you're a talented artist," whined Simon Snoot in a mocking voice, and a chorus of snickers followed. The bubble of happiness burst.

Henry picked up his lunchbox, which had clattered to the floor when he jumped after Simon. And as he picked it up, he saw that there was a small hole in the corner of it. Very, very carefully, he cracked open the lunchbox and peeked inside. There, sitting quietly between his grapes and carrot sticks, was a jungle-green spider.

He snapped the lunchbox shut again and plugged up the hole with a gum wrapper that had been wedged into the seat beside him.

He had a stowaway dragon disguised as a spider in his lunchbox. What now? Throw the lunchbox out the window? Tell his mother that an armadillo from the zoo had attacked the school bus and taken his lunch hostage? Let the dragon run wild around the town of Squashbuckle, while the only knight who could protect people from it was stuck in school all day? He couldn't do that. His chivalry wouldn't let him.

But what if he let it come to school with him? If his dragon got loose, it would be like everyone seeing his sketchbook. Worse: all of his wonderful creations would be tromping out freely in the world, for everyone to point at and laugh at and say, "What a weirdo that Henry Penwhistle is! Can you believe he drew *that*?" How he wished the dragon had just stayed on his door closed up in his room where it belonged! *Why* had it escaped? Why? Mr. Bruce was wrong—*letting it out* was the last thing in the world he wanted.

Henry wrapped his arms around his lunchbox and hugged it tightly to his chest. Somehow he would keep it hidden all day. He would keep the dragon from getting out, and when he got home from school he would find the bottle of superglue and glue that dragon to the door once and for all, so it could never come off. *That* was Sir Henry's quest. For today, at least.

When the bus pulled up to the school entrance, Henry waited until the rest of the kids spilled noisily into the parking lot, and then he stumbled down the aisle gripping his lunchbox fiercely.

"Be brave, Sir Henry," called Mr. Bruce as Henry was just about to step out the door.

Henry whirled around. Did the bus driver know? Had he guessed what secret Henry was holding?

"You have to be brave to be an artist." Mr. Bruce smiled and nodded at Henry's sketchbook. "It takes a fearless knight to imagine something and then let it out into the world. You never know what might happen to it. You never know what you might discover. Don't be scared! Go make something new!"

Henry carefully stepped off the bus and into the sunlight. He held a captive dragon under one arm and his quest under the other. *Be brave, Sir Henry. Be brave.*

Miss Pimpernel's Class

ON THE WAY TO CLASS, Henry dusted every crack and corner with his feather duster. And when he saw Simon Snoot's laughing face, he forgot all about the rules for being a good knight. He went over to Simon, held up the feather duster, and spun its handle between his two hands so furiously that Simon was covered with dirt and dead flies and spider webs before he even remembered to sneeze.

"Ha, ha! Take that, you Humuhumunukunukuapuaa!" said Oscar. Oscar was the shortest boy in the class, and he was so skinny that Simon Snoot could have tied him like a shoelace. But Oscar had the best insults, because his insults came out of the dictionary. That was his favorite: *hoo-moo-hoo-moo-noo-koo-noo-koo-ah-poo-ah-ah*. Twelve whole syllables. It means a kind of fish in Hawaii, but when you call someone that, they think you're putting a spell on them.

Henry looked at Oscar out of the corner of his eye. Seeing the Lego laboratory last night had reminded him of the dark memory he didn't want to think about. Did Oscar still think about it? But there was his best friend, insulting his mortal enemy. Everything was okay.

"Henry Penwhistle!" said Miss Pimpernel. "Do you intend to cover all of us with dust and spiders this morning? Go put your head on your desk for twenty minutes. If I see such behavior again, I'll send you to the principal's office."

Henry shuffled to his desk in shame.

Miss Pimpernel had hair the exact color of a beaver's teeth. She kept it wound into a tight ball at the back of her head, and in the light it shimmered like a copper penny. On her chin were precisely three freckles of the same color as her hair. Henry adored her. Her beaver-teeth hair made him happy, and so did her three freckles—and her smiles. Most of them, anyway. Miss Pimpernel had at least a hundred different kinds of smiles. Henry thought she must keep them in her gigantic purple purse and pull them out at night to count them, like a pirate grinning as she counted her pieces of silver. She could be his teacher for ten years and he would never finish learning the names of all of her smiles. Right now she was wearing her Be-Nice-to-Me-I-Haven't-Had-My-Coffee smile, which wasn't her happiest. Still, there were worse.

Yet in spite of all those smiles, looking at her often made him sad, and this was the reason: she had once been a superhero, but she had forgotten. Such things do happen. Henry knew there was a superhero hidden under her skin, because sometimes she could see Louie playing a video game behind his notebook *without even looking up from her desk*, and she could send a stapler rattling so fast across a bulletin board that her fist became a pale pink blur, and she could recite all of the state capitals in alphabetical order and not stumble once over *Des Moines*. And of course, most importantly, she could change her face into all sorts of new shapes just by putting on her different smiles. What other glorious things must she be capable of? What had happened to make her forget?

Henry sat down at his desk, which was next to Oscar's. Keeping his head low, he pulled tape and glue out of the desk. He wound the tape around and around his lunch box and smeared glue on all of the cracks. Then he scraped some dried gum off the bottom of his desk and smushed it into the latch.

Oscar watched him sympathetically. "Did your mom make you a spinach sandwich again?"

Henry placed the plastic prison carefully under his chair and whispered, "There was a dragon in my house this morning, and now it's inside the lunchbox."

Oscar's eyes opened wide. "How many teeth does it have?"

That's why Oscar was Henry's friend. He asked the right questions. Not "Are you crazy?" Not "How can a dragon fit in a lunchbox, stupid?" But "How many teeth does it have?"

"Good morning, boys and girls!" said Miss Pimpernel, with a You're-Going-to-Like-What-I'm-About-to-Tell-You smile on her face that outshone even her copper hair. "As you all know, we have to finish our art project for National Vegetable Week *this morning*! Our wonderful Lunch Lady just informed me that she is going to award a blue ribbon to the best Work of Art in the show, and the winning class will be announced during our *pizza party* at lunch today!"

The class exploded in applause—the kind of applause that only a pizza party can inspire.

Henry growled softly and glared down at his lunchbox. His mom always packed him a lunchbox full of healthy food on pizza party days. There probably *was* a spinach sandwich in there, unless the dragon-spider had eaten it. Why were the best and the worst things always green?

Miss Pimpernel took off her glasses and began to clean them quietly with a handkerchief. "Now I know," she continued, "you'll all want to draw the very *best bunnies* you can so that when we hang this in the cafeteria it will be greatly admired and applauded by one and all."

As the students shuffled around in their desks for paper and crayons, Henry looked at the enormous cardboard box sitting near the front of the classroom. It was big enough for Henry and Oscar to both fit into and still have enough room for a small dinosaur. Glued all over half of it were drawings of bunnies, all exactly the same shape and size, all covered with light brown fur, all pointing their little pink noses in the same direction, all in the process of devouring identical green lettuce leaves. The other half of the box was still bare and bunny-less.

Oh, Miss Pimpernel, Henry wanted to say, *don't you remember? Don't you remember when you could leap over skyscrapers and see through brick walls and twirl monsters around your little finger? How could you, of all people, make us draw bunnies?*

Henry took a piece of paper out of his desk, along with the cardboard shape of a bunny they were supposed to trace. Keeping his head low on his desk, he picked up a brown crayon. He laid the tip on the paper. He began to trace the ears.

The crayon trailed off and drew a space helmet.

No.

He scribbled over the space helmet.

He tried to trace again. The tail. A tail was easy. He should be able to draw a tail.

But as he looked at the paper, the little fluffy rabbit tail blurred, and all he could see was a bright orange fireball shooting out from the bunny like a rocket as it soared past Saturn.

No, no. Draw a tail.

Henry peeked at the other desks nearby. The other students were huddled over their papers, no doubt drawing perfect bunnies. Oscar had not started yet. He was still trying to sharpen his crayon to an exactly precise pointy point.

Marybeth raised her hand. "Miss Pimpernel, aren't *you* going to draw one?"

The other students looked up, and a wave of redness rippled up Miss Pimpernel's neck and splashed on her cheeks and made her three lonely freckles look like they were on fire. "Oh! Oh, no. No, Marybeth. I am a terrible artist. I could never make a bunny look like a real bunny. Believe me, you all don't want me ruining your beautiful box and spoiling the art show."

"But don't you like to draw?" persisted Marybeth, whose own bunny was so perfect that a carrot would probably beg to be eaten by it.

Miss Pimpernel laughed nervously and waved the question away with a graceful hand. "Goodness, I haven't drawn anything since I was a little girl! I'm just not creative like that. Some people have It, you know, and some people don't have It. And I definitely *don't*."

Suddenly a new thought crept into Henry's brain and

pinched him painfully. What was It, and what did it look like? If Miss Pimpernel, who used to be a superhero, didn't have It, and It was so important that without It she refused to draw even a bunny, then what if he didn't have It either? He too had a hard time making a bunny look like a real bunny. What if he was a terrible artist and just didn't know it? What if he ruined the box and spoiled the art show for everyone?

Henry pressed the crayon so hard against his paper that it broke, and a piece of it tumbled onto the floor. He bent down and reached under his chair to find the crayon. And then he forgot all about *It*-ness and whether or not he had it. Because under the chair was nothing. *Nothing.*

The lunchbox was gone.

His heart jumped as he peered around the room. He spotted the lunchbox lying on the floor beside the lockers. The tip of a green tail flickered out of a crack in the bottom, between two stretches of tape, and pushed against the floor until the lunchbox scooted forward. The tail did it again and again, and the lunchbox inched along quietly. The students' desks were all facing the other direction, so no one had noticed the unusual moving lunchbox except Henry.

Here he was, doing his best to draw the picture he was supposed to be drawing, while the picture he was supposed to erase was trying to escape! It wasn't fair!

Henry squeezed his armor against his chest to give himself courage, and then he raised his hand.

Miss Pimpernel looked up. "Henry, you're supposed to be silently thinking about your behavior. No raising your hand until the twenty minutes are up. Oscar, you have a very interesting shoebox on your desk today. Are those new shoes?"

"No, this is my pet octagon," said Oscar.

The faint glimmer of a Well-Aren't-You-Cute-but-of-Course-You-Don't-Know-What-You're-Talking-About smile tugged at the teacher's mouth. "There's no such animal as an octagon, Oscar. An octagon is a shape with eight sides, like this." She drew it on the board:

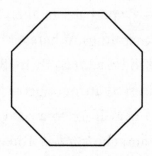

"This was on our math test, remember?"

"That's not an octagon. That's a *fossil* of an octagon," said Oscar. "An octagon is hairy and eats circles. That's why I keep it in a shoebox. One time it escaped and ate eleven dollars and forty-five cents—in *nickels*."

Henry watched his lunchbox inch over to the back corner of the classroom, where the children's coats hung on pegs. The side of the lunchbox facing upward began to buckle and bulge, as if something sharp inside was trying to get out.

Miss Pimpernel pushed her large round glasses further up on her nose and peered to the back of the room. "Yes, Jade?" she said. "Do you have a question? You're looking sparkly this morning."

Jade Longswallow had moved to Squashbuckle two weeks ago, and already Henry was suspicious that she was a government spy—or perhaps an alien life form sent on a mission to kidnap earthlings. Wherever he and Oscar were, she always seemed to be *watching* them. She stood alone on the playground, dressed in outrageously colorful outfits, talking out loud to herself (or to a secret phone hidden in her hair barrette), and she *watched*. Today she was wearing a fuzzy purple scarf, green pants rolled up to her knees, suspenders, and soccer cleats. Her nails were painted ten different colors of glitter. "I have a pet paperclip," she said loudly. "It's like a silvery snake all curled up."

Oscar looked unimpressed. A *paperclip* was nothing compared to a real live octagon. He pulled the shoebox closer and opened the lid slightly, dropping a round breath mint inside. There was a soft *crunch*.

"Jade, a paperclip is not a pet," said Miss Pimpernel. "But this is a good time to learn about similes: *sim-i-leeeeees*. A simile uses the word *like* to compare one thing to another. Can anyone think of a simile starting with 'The sunset is like . . . '? Louie? You aren't playing a video game in the classroom, are you?"

Louie's head, shoulders, and hands were all buried behind a notebook fort he had built on his desk. There was a rattling of something in his lap, and his eyes peeked guiltily over the top of his notebook at Miss Pimpernel. "No, ma'am."

"I know one, Miss Pimpernel," said Simon Snoot loudly. Simon always had the answer, even when he didn't. "The sunset is like the sun sinking lower in the sky until everything is dark."

"Well," Miss Pimpernel said, "that's *true*, Simon, though it isn't *exactly* comparing the sunset to something else . . ."

"Is there going to be a test on this?"

"There's a test on *everything*, Simon," Miss Pimpernel sighed.

Henry, meanwhile, couldn't take his eyes off the lunchbox. The bulge on the side of it grew taller and sharper, until the object inside finally poked through. He recognized it at once. Why oh why oh why had he ever drawn a coat rack on his bedroom door? He had liked the way it was like a spooky tree with ghosts hanging from the branches. Now he wished they were ghosts after all. Because the coat rack bursting out of the lunchbox and growing up, *up*, UP was much, *much*, MUCH more frightening.

The rest of the students were still facing the front of the classroom, away from the transformation happening behind them. Miss Pimpernel turned to write the word SIMILE on the board and didn't notice anything amiss. *How can she see Louie's video game and not see THIS?* Henry thought in frustration.

"Does anyone else have a simile for us?" Miss Pimpernel asked.

Marybeth answered, "The sunset is, like, so pretty behind my house, and I, like, so much want to learn how to paint so I can paint things like the sunset."

"The sunset is like the sun got a cold and wiped its nose all over the sky," said Trina. The class crowed with laughter, and Trina shyly hid her eyes behind a bag of marshmallows so that all you could see of her were the corners of her big grin stretching from one ear to the other.

Drew, who had been quietly trying to blow a red kazoo in the corner of the classroom, let out an unmusical squeak and turned as red as his kazoo. More laughter.

Miss Pimpernel took off her glasses again and peered at the perfectly round lenses as if her patience were hidden somewhere inside the little glass circles.

Henry wanted to tell his teacher all kinds of similes about sunsets. He wanted to say that a sunset is like a huge red-hot bowling ball that smashed into a rainbow and melted it. He wanted her to shine her My-Goodness-You-Are-a-Brilliant-Boy smile on him. But there were more important matters to deal with. The dragon-coat-rack was biting the children's coats on the wall as if they were lasagna noodles, when it spotted the Art Project at the front of the classroom and began to creep towards it. Henry raised his hand again and waved it frantically in the air.

"Henry," Miss Pimpernel said, "if you raise your hand one more time, I'll have to stop smiling."

Henry scrunched down low into his seat and raised his foot.

Miss Pimpernel sighed. "Yes, Henry?"

Henry opened his mouth, and his voice did what his voice always did when he opened his mouth at school: it shrank. "The coat rack is a dragon," he whispered hoarsely. Stupid voice. He pointed, and all eyes turned to the back of the classroom. The coat rack froze in its place, looking as guilty as a coat rack can look.

"That's not a simile, Henry. That's a metaphor: *met-uh-forrrr*. A metaphor is when you say that something *is* something else, but what you really mean is that it is *like* something else. This long pole of the coat rack is kind of *like* the long tail of a dragon." Miss Pimpernel walked over to the coat rack, which had grown to its full height and was looking as if it had always stood there. But when Miss Pimpernel turned her head back to the class for a moment, the long pole rippled as if it were going to whip its tail

around her. The students began to wiggle nervously in their seats. "And the two coats hanging from these two arms of the coat rack are *like* a dragon's wings." As she turned back to the class again, the coats rose and flapped quietly. The classroom erupted in gasps. "And these two smaller empty arms at the top are *like* two horns. But of course," she finished, and smiled her brightest I'm-Teaching-You-a-Very-Important-Lesson smile, "it isn't really a dragon, is it? Because *dragons don't exist.*"

And then, for the first time in his life, Henry said something in front of the whole class in a voice louder than a whisper. In fact, he yelled it at the top of his lungs:

"LOOK OUT, MISS PIMPERNEL! THE COAT RACK IS ABOUT TO EAT YOU!"

He jumped up from his chair and leaped to save Miss Pimpernel, but he was more like a lumpy, alumi-num-foil-covered bowling ball that smashed into a rainbow and bounced off again. And several things happened at once.

Miss Pimpernel toppled over onto the floor, and her glasses went flying across the room.

The coat rack stopped looking *like* a dragon and turned

into a real live dragon, and the rest of the students began screaming and ran to the other side of the classroom.

Marybeth tripped and knocked Oscar's shoebox off his desk, and he scrambled to the floor after it.

Oscar yelled, "Where's my octagon?"

Miss Pimpernel yelled, "Where are my glasses?"

Then there was a loud CRUNCH CRUNCH.

CHAPTER 6

DRAGON SMILES

"I'M BLIND without my glasses!" cried Miss Pimpernel. She was squinting and crawling on her knees, patting the floor with her hands. To Henry's horror, she crawled right through the dragon's legs.

But the dragon was not in the slightest bit interested in Miss Pimpernel. It spread its wings widely, flew over the heads of the students, and landed right on top of the bunny-covered box at the front of the classroom. With a sad groan of defeated cardboard and the squish of paper lettuce, the class's Vegetable Week Art Project crumpled under the weight of Henry Penwhistle's fearsome dragon. The class screamed again. The dragon sat proudly, its green rump on a lump of crayon-colored bunnies, and waited to be greatly admired and applauded by one and all.

But no one was clapping. For several seconds, all Henry could see were arms and legs and wide-open eyes and wide-open mouths as his classmates tried to figure out which way to run. Squeezing between them, Oscar reached under the teacher's desk and pulled out a pair of eyeglass frames. The two lenses were gone—two delicious, crunchy *circles*. But the octagon was nowhere to be found.

"No need for all of that screaming," said Miss Pimpernel calmly. "I'm all right! No broken bones. Don't worry about me. Just a little tumble, that's all. Has anyone seen my glasses?"

"You can have mine, Miss Pimpernel," said Norman Treble, one of the Treble triplets, who all wore glasses. (It would be so easy, Henry often thought, for them to put one shirt on and pretend they were a three-headed monster with twelve eyes that could see all the way to outer space, and then charge people money to tell them what was happening on Neptune, and gobble up the ones who didn't pay. That's what he would do if he were lucky enough to be a triplet and have two other brothers with identical heads who wore so many glasses.)

But for three identical boys who could see all the way to Neptune, they could never think in the same direction.

"You can have mine, Miss Pimpernel," said Norman Treble, grabbing his brothers Nelson and Neville by the elbows and running toward the teacher.

"That's a dragon!" said Nelson Treble, grabbing Neville and Norman by the thumbs and running to where the dragon wasn't.

"Last one to the fire alarm is a peacock!" said Neville Treble, grabbing Norman and Nelson by the ears and running toward the fire alarm.

And so, instead of going anywhere, they became a three-headed tangle of shirts and shoes on the floor. And then Walter tripped over them (Walter was always tripping), and then six other students fell on top in a rush of elbows and thumbs and ears trying to escape. Over their heads leaped Marybeth, her pink dress swoooooooping around her like the wings of a beautiful butterfly. She landed beside Miss Pimpernel on the floor and curled up into a pink cocoon.

"Is that you, Marybeth?" the teacher asked, blindly patting Marybeth's cheeks. "You sweet thing, help me look for my glasses . . . "

The dragon bared its claws. The class squealed.

It swiveled its tail. The class shrieked.

"Now that's enough hooting and hollering and rough-housing! I think you all have had enough drawing for the day, art show or no art show. If I can just find my spare pair of glasses, we'll start math." Miss Pimpernel stood up and stumbled across the room with her nose buried in her gigantic purple purse.

She tripped over the Treble triplets. The purse flew out of her hands, landed on one of the dragon's horns, and split open, and a hundred smiles tumbled out onto the dragon's face.

There are many things in this world that do not belong. A volcano does not belong in a bathroom. The Indian Ocean does not belong in Iowa. Ketchup does not belong on chocolate cake. But most of all, *most* of all, a teacher's smiles do not belong on the face of a fearsome dragon.

When the You-Are-the-Apple-of-My-Eye smile is stretched between two glittering dragon eyes, believe me, you do not want to be the apple.

The Read-This-Book-You'll-Like-It-I-Promise smile is not quite as tempting when it is hanging from the end of two smoking dragon nostrils.

And no one in that class would ever forget, till their dying day, the sparkle of the dragon's teeth as it smiled the I-Know-You-Didn't-Really-Lose-Your-Homework-in-a-Hippopotamus-Stampede smile.

Simon Snoot crossed his arms and rolled his eyes. "That's so dumb," he said. Only he and Louie had not yet moved from their seats. Louie was still buried behind his notebook fortress, playing his video game. For one brief moment the students turned their eyes from the dragon to Simon. "It's *obviously* not *real*," he said with a smirk. "Duh. It's just someone playing a trick. Look at those wings—they're all crooked, like someone made them who didn't even know what wings look like. And the horn looks like a bad haircut. Hey, you in there! Take off your costume and go home!" The dragon swung its head angrily towards Simon, and all of the teacher smiles fell off its face. But Simon merely jumped up from his seat and flapped his arms and squealed in a high-pitched, mocking voice, "Don't eat me! I'm not a human, I'm a duck. Dragons don't like ducks. See?" He waddled on the floor and flapped his elbows. "QUACK QUACK QUACK! Louie, Louie, save me!"

"Shhh, I've almost beat level twenty-five!" said Louie.

"But *look*—" screamed Marybeth.

"Just a *second*!" yelled Louie, his fingers flying over the game controls.

Drew pointed his kazoo at the dragon and blew music out of it that sounded the way a zipper would sound if a zipper could sing. The dragon smiled again. Drew dropped the kazoo and hid his head under a trashcan.

"Don't eat my marshmallows," sobbed Trina, grasping the bag tightly in her hands and backing as far away from the dragon as possible.

"You can eat my trumpet," said Katie generously. "Then I won't have to go to band practice."

Simon Snoot's face was growing red with annoyance. "See, Miss Pimpernel isn't scared. 'Cause it's *not real*. Dragons aren't real. That's what she said. There's no test on *dragons*."

"It *is* real," said Jade quietly from the back of the classroom. "Just *look* at it."

Miss Pimpernel wasn't even listening, much less looking. She was still squinting at the floor, hastily gathering up the contents of her purse and stuffing them into her pockets.

"Oh dear, oh dear," she murmured, picking up something that was either a secret superhero weapon or a nose hair trimmer. "How embarrassing."

The others students stared at Miss Pimpernel, then at Simon Snoot, then at Jade, then at the dragon, and then back at Miss Pimpernel. Confusion flittered across their faces.

Henry watched his classmates in despair. They were all useless in an adventure. He would like them so much better if they wore shiny helmets and said things like "Forsooth!" once in a while. Maybe he should just leave the dragon to eat them all for lunch and go find a goblin or a heffalump or a vampire bunny to fight instead. Why not? What was stopping him?

Chivalry.

That's what you get for putting on armor in the morning. You have to defend those who are in trouble, protect those who are afraid, fight for the right, and eat your spinach.

Oscar, at least, was standing ready, as he always was, with a pencil in his pocket and a tuft of hair sticking out crookedly above his ear. He was ready to follow Henry to outer space or to the bottom of the sea or to the muddiest swamp of the darkest forest. And if he occasionally forgot what they were doing and stopped to collect a soil sample, or inspect a strange bug, or count rocks, Henry always had something in his backpack to remind his friend what *adventure* really meant.

Henry opened his backpack and fumbled around inside for something to throw. He pulled out the eraser and hurled it at the dragon, thinking to distract the beast by hitting it on the nose. But instead, the eraser went straight through the dragon's right foreclaw, leaving nothing behind but a *poof* of shimmering green dust.

The dragon looked at the empty space where his foreclaw had been and howled in surprise. Fear was smeared across its green face as it stared back at Henry. Fear and something else—the look of someone who has been betrayed.

The eraser had *erased* it—or at least part of it—just like a chalk drawing on a door. And then a tremendous idea burst into Henry's mind. His mother had asked him to erase the dragon, and he had agreed. And the very next morning, the dragon had escaped. That was it! It didn't want to be erased!

Maybe it didn't want to be replaced by a bunny. Maybe it didn't want to be stuck on a door at home when an Art

Project was going to be greatly admired and applauded at school. Maybe it didn't steal all the other shapes on the door because it was greedy—maybe the dragon thought it was saving them.

Whatever the *maybes*, Henry's task was clear now. "Oscar, pick up the eraser!" Oscar did and prepared to throw it, but the dragon spread its wings again and flew out the door of the classroom and down the hallway. Henry ran after it. "Let's go!"

"Wait, I have to find my octagon! I think it escaped!"

"We'll look for it on the way," urged Henry.

Oscar yelled, "Miss Pimpernel, we have to go to the BATHROOM!" He and Henry dashed out the door into the hallway. "Wait!" said Oscar again, stopping and grabbing Henry's arm. "I have to be a knight first. I can't go off fighting a dragon unless I'm a knight."

Henry solemnly touched the feather duster to Oscar's head. "I dub thee Sir Oscar Rockbottom! Now come on, hurry."

"Wait! I don't have a suit of armor. What kind of knight doesn't wear a suit of armor?" Oscar's mother made him wear shirts with buttons all the way from his neck to the part that was tucked into his pants, and the kind of shoes that weren't supposed to get dirty. But usually after a day with Henry, Oscar was missing several buttons, and the bottom of his shirt was hanging down to his knees, and half the Sahara Desert was stuck to his shoes.

"We're chasing a dragon who wears disguises," said Henry, "so you can be a knight disguised as an ordinary boy. It will confuse the dragon." He gave the feather duster to Oscar and raised the eraser high in the air. "Sally forth!"

"*Sally?*" said Oscar. "My name is not *Sally.*"

"It means 'Let's go!' in knight language."

"Oh." Oscar raised the feather duster. "Oscar forth!"

Henry raised the eraser again. "Henry forth!"

"Wait! I want to be a knight too!" said a voice behind them. Oscar and Henry turned around and looked in surprise at Jade, who stood with her glittery-fingered hands on her hips. Her chin was high, her eyes were sparkling, and her fuzzy scarf swirled around her neck like a wild purple cloud.

"You can't be a knight," Henry said. "You're a *girl!*" He added under his breath, *Not to mention an alien spy who's trying to kidnap us.*

"So?" she said, holding her chin even higher.

"So . . ." Henry knew there was a really good reason, but he couldn't seem to remember it.

"So," said Oscar, "knights are called *Sirs*, and whoever heard of a Sir *Girl*?"

Jade sighed. "Oh, Oscar, you're such a cliché."

"You don't even know what a *klee-shay* is!" said Oscar, because he didn't.

"Tell me, then," said Jade.

"It's—it's a kind of insect that lived a million gazillion years ago."

"No, it's not. A cliché is something you've heard over and over and over again until it's just silly. See? You don't know *every* word in the dictionary."

"I know the good ones," mumbled Oscar.

"My mom always says to me, 'Jade, you can be whatever you want to be when you grow up. But whatever you do, don't be a cliché.'"

Having his vocabulary corrected did not put Oscar in a good mood. "Come on," he said to Henry and started to run down the hallway.

"Wait!" said Jade. "I could be your bard and travel by

your side playing a harp and singing epic poems about your heroic exploits against fearsome enemies!"

"You don't have a harp," said Henry.

Jade tossed her hair back and started singing:

> *O hear this humble poet sing her story*
> *Of brave Sir Henry's quest for fame and glory!*
> *A noble knight he was, like all his ilk—*
> *Charm trickled from his chin like dribbled milk!*

Henry wasn't sure exactly what she had just said, but her words sounded like trumpets. They echoed inside his chest, making him feel taller and braver. He could almost see them, scrawled in gold letters across the pages of his quest.

Oscar raised his feather duster again. "The dragon is getting away! Oscar forth!"

Jade sang even louder:

> *His staunch companion, Sir Oscar Rockbottom,*
> *Fought boldly too until a dragon got him.*

"Hey!" said Oscar.

Henry looked at Jade for a moment, wishing he could

hear the trumpets again. Then he turned away and raised the eraser. "Henry forth!"

And they went forth, leaving Jade to sing epic poems by herself. But Henry could still hear the echo of her voice long after they had left her, as if her song was bouncing along behind them, following.

CHAPTER 7

THE SAFEST SCHOOL
IN THE COUNTY

LA MUNCHA Elementary School was perfectly round. There was one long hallway going around the whole school, with classrooms on the outer ring and classrooms on the inner ring. The very center of the school—the hole in the middle of the donut—was the cafeteria. A few smaller hallways led to the school entrances.

As Henry and Oscar crept around the curve of the main hallway, they had no trouble finding the path the escaped octagon had taken. A clock had disappeared from a wall, a doorknob had been bitten off, a cart had lost its wheels. Everywhere they looked, round things were missing— eaten. But the dragon was harder to track.

Suddenly Henry stopped and pointed to a mysterious puddle on the floor. "Look!"

"What is it?" whispered Oscar.

"Elementary, my dear Watson," whispered Henry.

"My name is not *Watson*. It's *Oscar*. Why do you keep forgetting?"

"That's detective language. And this is a penguin's footprint. That means there was a penguin here—a dragon *disguised* as a penguin—and its trail is still wet."

"Maybe the iceberg it was floating on melted."

"It was an igloo. I drew the penguin inside an igloo." Henry pulled out his sketchbook and showed Oscar the drawing.

Oscar frowned skeptically. "Penguins don't live in igloos. Eskimos build igloos, and they aren't in Antarctica like the penguins are."

"Well, they're both cold. I bet a penguin *would* live in an igloo if it could."

"So where did it go?"

But that wasn't the only question, as Henry knew. Was the penguin still a penguin? Or was the dragon now disguised as some other shape from his door?

Henry and Oscar tiptoed down the hall. Except for the low hum of teachers' voices, the hallway was quiet. "Don't let anyone see you," whispered Henry. "And if we get separated, we can talk through the walkie-talkies hidden in our shoes."

"Hidden in our shoes?"

"All spies have walkie-talkies in their shoes so they can have secret conversations. Why do you think they're called *walkie*-talkies?"

"So we're spies now? I thought we were detectives. I mean, I thought we were knights."

"We're knights who are also being spies."

Oscar stared at Henry in frustration and raised his voice. "How am I supposed to know what to do if I can't even figure out what I am? You're as confused as the dragon! I'm not going another step until you pick *one* thing to be and stick to it."

"Shhhhh!" shushed Henry. "Okay, okay. We're knights . . . who are moving very secretly."

"Okay. Sorry," mumbled Oscar. "I'm just worried about my octagon. It never would have escaped if your dragon hadn't scared everyone and made the shoebox get knocked over. Someone could step on it. Or it could eat too much and get sick. Hey, if something that eats meat is a carnivore and something that eats plants is an herbivore, then is something that eats round things a circlivore?"

But Henry's mind was on other matters. "Do you think maybe we should have let Jade come with us?"

Oscar stared at him as if he had just spoken platypus language. "Of course not! What do we need *her* for?"

"It's just that—" Henry felt silly, but her words had seemed so—so *golden.* They were still bouncing around inside of him, and he liked it. "Yeah, you're right. I can make my own epic poems. Like this . . .

There once was a knight named Sir Henry
And he fought a dragon who was really hungry.

Somehow that didn't sound right. There were no trumpets.

"You're a nut," said Oscar.

"I am not a nut."

"Hey, I've got an idea. If we can find out what kind of roar a dragon's *mother* makes, then we can sneak into Principal Bunk's office and use the intercom to broadcast dragon-mother sounds around the whole school. And the dragon will miss its mother and come looking for her, and then we can catch it."

"No, I've got a better idea," said Henry. "You can keep being a knight, but I need to be a superhero for a minute."

Oscar looked doubtful. "What is your superpower?"

"I can read people's minds. But only on Fridays. And only when I'm wearing my supersocks."

"Okay then, what am I thinking?"

"You're wondering if I can read your mind."

Oscar's eyes opened wide. "You're right! Well, who else's mind are you going to read?"

Henry sat down on the floor, squeezed one of his super-sock-wearing feet, and closed his eyes. *If I were a dragon*, he thought, *if I were a dragon who jumped off a door and I was running from someone with an eraser, if I were a dragon who wanted to be admired and applauded by one and all, what would I do? Where would I go? What would I be?*

He took out his sketchbook and flipped through the pages. Suddenly one page made his heart freeze. "Can I see?" said Oscar, straining to look over Henry's shoulder.

But Henry jerked away. "Wait a minute. My superpowers

need space." He stared at the page in front of him, and a sick feeling rolled around in his stomach like an ocean of socks. Green dragon-poop socks.

It was a picture of a dinosaur, with spikes on its back and outstretched wings and with its mouth open wide, teeth bared, getting ready to bite into its prey—a little boy with a tucked-in buttoned-up shirt and never-get-dirty shoes. The dinosaur was about to eat Oscar.

He had forgotten about this picture, and now the whole dark memory came flooding back. He had drawn it last week after the Big Fight, the biggest they had ever had. He remembered so clearly the way it had ended:

"You're a *pig face!*"

"Well, you're a *blobfish face!*"

"Well, you're a *skunk face!*"

"Well, you're a *trout-snouted putrefied armadillo face!*" That was Oscar's insult, and Henry knew he was beaten at the worst-face war. Oscar always won when it came to words, because Henry thought it was silly to interrupt a battle to look up a word like *pyootreefied* in the dictionary. So instead, he grabbed the dusty dictionary off his shelf and knocked over Oscar's Lego laboratory with it. And so Oscar had smeared finger paint all over the drawing on Henry's door, the drawing that had started the whole argument in the first place.

Henry didn't want to think about how it had started. Even now, a week later, the memory still hurt.

It had been an epic battle, and after Oscar stomped home, Henry had wiped the paint smears off the door and won the battle with his chalk, making sure that the dinosaur was especially terrifying and that Oscar's face was white with fear. When he was satisfied with his revenge, he had copied the dinosaur into his sketchbook along with all of his other adventures.

The next day, they were best friends again. And Henry had drawn something else, and another thing, and another thing, and he had forgotten all about this angry picture.

And now, as he looked at it, he felt like the worst person who was ever born on the whole earth. The worst knight, the worst artist, the worst friend. If the dragon turned into the dinosaur, the dinosaur would eat Oscar—and it would be all Henry's fault.

He had to stop it. He had to erase the dragon before that happened.

"Let me see!" said Oscar.

"NO!" said Henry and snapped the book shut. The word came out more sharply than he meant, and Oscar fell back with a hurt expression on his face.

His pig face. His skunk face. His wonderful best friend face.

They heard the rumble of footsteps and the murmur of voices. Henry grabbed Oscar's arm and pulled him under a table. Principal Bunk was walking toward them.

Unlike Miss Pimpernel, Principal Bunk only had one smile, and he wore it all the time. It was as if he had gone to the smile store, picked out the most cheerful one he could find, and then glued it onto his villainous face. He was smiling now as he led a man and a woman down the hall. Henry recognized them as people Principal Bunk called Bored Members. They occasionally visited the school, wearing dark suits and even darker glasses, so that they could stare at everyone, but no one could ever quite see whom they were watching. And they wrote things down in notebooks, and listened in a way that made you squirm.

The Bored Man and the Bored Woman were not smiling.

"I assume, Principal Bunk," said the Bored Woman in a bored voice, "that you have met all of the new safety regulations?"

"I can assure you," chirped the principal, "La Muncha Elementary School is the safest school in the county. It's an emergency-free zone. Absolutely unbreakable windows! Doors so thick a herd of elephants couldn't barge through! Fireproof carpets! Sprinklers in every room! Perfectly polished doorknobs! There is nothing we would not do to protect the well-being, comfort, health, and happiness of the beloved pupils entrusted to our care."

"But Principal Bunk—" said the Bored Man.

"We're sorry to say—" said the Bored Woman.

"The Bored has decided that there will no longer be a need for doorknobs."

"Yes, doorknobs have been cut out of the budget."

Principal Bunk stopped walking and swallowed so hard that Henry could see the swallow slide all the way down his necktie. "Doorknobs?"

"Studies have shown that doorknobs will not help students do any better on tests. Therefore, all doorknobs must be turned in to the Bored by next week."

A trickle of sweat rolled down Principal Bunk's cheek. He wiped it away with his sleeve. "Of course. Who needs doorknobs? Nasty, germ-covered things. May I . . . may I ask what else has been cut out of the budget?"

The Bored Man looked down at his notebook. "Pink erasers . . . zoology . . . spatulas . . . and . . ."

"The letter *Z*," finished the Bored Woman. "No one will really need *Z* anymore, once zoology is gone."

"But not—*principals*? You're not cutting principals out of the budget, are you?"

The Bored Man lowered his nose and squinted at Principal Bunk over the top of his dark glasses. "No. Well—not yet."

And right before Henry's eyes, Principal Bunk shrank. Perhaps shrinking was his supervillain power, but at that moment, standing beside the Bored Man, he looked less like a supervillain and more like a lump of melting ice with a glued-on smile. For the first time in all of his school days, Henry felt sorry for the principal.

The Bored Woman checked her notebook again. "Now, let's talk about National Vegetable Week. How will La Muncha be observing this educational event?"

"Well . . . er . . . we're holding a . . . um . . . it's an excellent idea, really . . ." The principal fidgeted with his necktie and scratched his bald head nervously.

"Principal Bunk, Principal Bunk!" Mrs. Lightfoot, the gym teacher, sprinted down the hall and slid to a stop in front of the Bored Members. "Something strange seems to be happening to the children! They are all *seeing* things— *unusual* things. I came into the gym to find the volleyballs completely flattened, and the students swore a *boa constrictor wearing a space helmet* had squeezed the air out of them!"

The principal and the Bored Man gasped, while the Bored Woman looked like she was about to faint. Mrs. Lightfoot said quickly, "Squeezed the air out of the *balls*, I mean—not the *students*, thank goodness!" The Bored Members sighed and wrote something down in their notebooks. Another trickle of sweat dripped off the principal's nose.

"When I walked into the gym," the gym teacher continued, "they were all singing, 'Oh no, oh no, it's up to my toe, it's up to my toe!' and I nearly swallowed my whistle! The students were singing, I mean, not the balls. They were flat. The balls, I mean. The students sang very nicely." She took a deep breath. "And that's not all! Mrs. Polar's class told her a *penguin* waddled down the hallway while they were taking a math test. A *green* penguin. And three kindergartners claim to have seen the *Tooth Fairy* trying to pull the teeth out of Mr. Addler's alligator puppet. Do you think we should line up everyone in the school and have their vision checked? Perhaps there's an eye epidemic!"

"Are all those things the dragon?" whispered Oscar.

"Yes," Henry groaned, "it's turning into the pictures I drew on my door."

Oscar snickered. "You drew the *Tooth Fairy*?"

"Carrying a sword made from a walrus tooth!" retorted Henry. This whole day was beginning to make him feel as if his brain were an underwear drawer and someone had pinned the underwear up on the wall for everyone to see.

The Bored Woman kept writing in her notebook. The Bored Man clucked his tongue. "I do hope, Principal Bunk, that this is not a *typical day* at La Muncha Elementary School. We wouldn't want an entire generation of children to grow up believing in green penguins and helmet-wearing snakes, would we?"

"Of course not, of course not!" said the principal, and his smile spread so wide it nearly squeezed his cheeks into his ears, but it was not a happy smile. No, not at all. "The remedy for green penguins is, quite simply, more spelling tests, tighter shoelaces, and long, firm conversations about what is TRUE and what is NOT."

"But Principal Bunk—" began Mrs. Lightfoot.

Just then, there was such a clickety-clackety-clumpty-clump-rumpus that Henry thought an army of Tin Men was invading from Oz. But instead, a tall figure draped in a jungle-green cape came skipping around the corner, straddling a broom. In one hand it held a fire-breathing jack-o'-lantern with a frightening Catch-Me-Now! smile. The other arm, the *right* one, the one hooked around the broom, had no hand at all. The figure in the cape was not smiling. There was nothing above its neck to smile with.

"What is *that*?" whispered Oscar.

"The Headless Horseman," groaned Henry.

"Why is it headless?"

"Because I can't draw faces."

"Why is it riding a broom?"

"Because I can't draw horses either."

The Headless Horseman skipped down the hall and out of sight again. Henry watched the adults closely to see what they had noticed. The trouble with most grown-ups, Henry had learned, is that they paid attention to the wrong things. They spotted the peanut butter sandwich you accidently stuffed into your pocket, but they missed the Martian landing a spaceship in the backyard.

"I seem to remember," said Mrs. Lightfoot, rubbing her eyes, "that the fifth graders are practicing their Halloween play today. I'll go ask Mr. Furble if he can keep his actors behind closed doors."

"Oh, no need, Mrs. Lightfoot," said the principal. "That was the new janitor, I believe. Highly skilled with a broom, they say."

Who ever heard of a Headless Janitor? thought Henry, exasperated. *Nobody's paying attention. I have to do something.*

He remembered the orange scrawl of chivalry in his armor: **TELL THE TRUTH**.

Tell the truth? But the grown-ups would never believe him!

I'm a knight. I'm a brave knight.

Brave enough not to be believed?

Henry took a deep breath, leaped out from underneath the table, and drew his eraser. Oscar followed him with the feather duster. "It's a dragon, Principal Bunk!" yelled Henry. "I drew it and it came to life but I promise I'm going to erase it so just please tell everyone not to panic."

He knew instantly that he had made a mistake. The Bored Man and the Bored Woman turned their dark glasses first toward him, then back to Principal Bunk. They cleared their throats. They tapped their pens against their notebooks. The principal's smiling cheeks turned a deep shade of purple. His smile quivered and almost cracked. But then, he laughed. He turned toward the Bored Members and laughed.

"Cute kid, that Henry Penwhistle," said the principal, slapping his side and guffawing a little too loudly and nervously. "He's always making a joke." And the Bored Man and the Bored Woman chuckled with their unsmiling mouths.

This time, it was Henry who shrank. He could feel himself sinking into his armor, growing smaller under the weight of their laughter.

Oscar stepped closer to Henry. He glared at the principal and hooked his arm around the elbow of Henry's raincoat. "*Humuhumunukunukuapuaa*," he growled under his breath, so that only Henry could hear.

CHAPTER 8
THE HUNGRY HAT

THERE WAS A SWELLING thunder of footsteps, and Henry turned to see his class coming down the hall. They were whispering nervously to each other, and Marybeth's eyes were puffy from crying, but when they saw the little group around the principal, they grew silent and stared at Henry suspiciously.

Miss Pimpernel (who had evidently found her spare pair of glasses) swept by with hardly a glance at him or Oscar. "Principal Bunk, may I speak with you for a moment? Class, please proceed to the library." She whispered something in the principal's ear, and Henry thought he heard his own name. He sank even deeper into his armor.

From up ahead, around the curving hallway, they heard the voice of the librarian, Mr. Boolean. "Boys and girls, what a surprise we have today! Does anyone know who was the sixteenth president of the United States?"

Henry and Oscar joined the rear of the line, right after Jade. She didn't look at them but stood as straight and proud as a flagpole, her fuzzy scarf unfurling behind her as she marched ahead of them.

Henry wanted to say something to her, but he couldn't think of any words. They had left her behind when she wanted to be a knight. Surely she didn't think he was a hero anymore.

But then, why would anyone think he was?

As Miss Pimpernel spoke with the principal, the class filed into the library. Mr. Boolean stood beside a strange visitor. It was Abraham Lincoln himself—long face, beard, tall black stovepipe hat, and all. Except his hat wasn't black. It was jungle-green.

Oscar let out a yelp and dropped the feather duster.

"See? I told you I can't draw faces," whispered Henry.

"No kidding! Is that a nose? And look—he doesn't have a right hand! It's still erased!"

"Four score and seven years ago," said the fake Abraham Lincoln, except that when he said it, it sounded like a metal snake had rusted in the rain and was hissing into a microphone that was crackling with static. "Four *sssss*core and *sssss*even year*sssss* ago . . ."

That is not Abraham Lincoln! Henry wanted to say, but he clapped his hand over his mouth before the words could come out. He had tried to warn Miss Pimpernel *and* Principal Bunk, and look what happened. He couldn't bear to try and fail again, not in front of the whole class. What should he do? He peeked inside of his armor.

SPEAK UP, SCAREDY PANTS, said the orange crayon words scrawled across the pocket lining. Orange was such a rude color. Henry decided to throw the orange crayon out the window when he got home.

"Welcome, welcome, come sit down!" said Mr. Boolean as the students gathered in a circle on the library floor. "A man from the Historical Society came to school dressed up as President Lincoln, and he's going to teach us a lesson about the Civil War."

Henry did not know what man from the Historical Society was *supposed* to come to the school that day, but this was definitely not the right one.

"Four *sssscore* and *sssseven yearsssss* ago. . . ," continued the fake Abraham Lincoln. "Can *sssssomeone pleasssssse sssssshow me where the cafeteria isssssss?*"

"Why does Abraham Lincoln want to go to the cafeteria?" whispered Oscar.

"I don't know," whispered Henry. "He's probably hungry. Tell them he's a dragon."

"He's a dragon!" Oscar yelled. He was never shy about yelling, no matter who laughed.

At the word *dragon*, the class looked at Oscar in alarm (except for Simon Snoot, who rolled his eyes), and Marybeth began to whimper. But Abraham Lincoln didn't roar; instead, he reached down with his left hand and gently ruffled her hair. Then he winked at her, and Marybeth smiled, and the rest of the students relaxed. This man was obviously nothing like the terrifying creature in the classroom.

"No, Oscar," said Mr. Boolean, "Abraham Lincoln is not a dragon. He was one of America's best and noblest presidents! Look, I'll show you a photograph and you can see for yourself." Mr. Boolean turned around and began leafing through a large book on his desk.

While the librarian's back was turned, the fake Abraham Lincoln took his hat off and set it on the floor. The he picked up Trina, popped her inside his hat, and put it back on his head. The muffled voice of Trina inside the hat said, "Hey!" and she giggled. Simon Snoot let out a loud guffaw, and the rest of the class snickered. Dragon-Lincoln grinned.

Henry had forgotten Abraham Lincoln was so *tall*. He was like a bearded, bow-tied tower, with a left hand so large and strong it had plucked Trina from the carpet as if she were as light as a marshmallow. Henry looked sternly at the man with the huge hat and the badly drawn nose. "*Tell the truth*," he whispered. "Tell them you're really a dragon." But secretly, silently, inside of his own head, he was saying, *Don't-turn-into-a-dinosaur-don't-turn-into-a-dinosaur-don't-turn-into-a-dinosaur.* He edged a little bit in front of Oscar so that he was standing between his friend and the imposter.

"Oh, good grief," said Simon Snoot, "there he goes about that dragon again. It's *Abraham Lincoln*. Can't you see?"

The other students looked doubtfully at the visitor. He certainly didn't *look* like a dragon. In fact, he looked very nice indeed, except for the crooked nose and the missing hand.

"Father, I cannot tell a lie," crackled the fake Abraham Lincoln. "I did chop down the cherry tree."

"Abraham Lincoln didn't say that," said Oscar. "George Washington did . . . I think."

"Aha!" said Mr. Boolean. "Which president said he couldn't tell a lie about chopping down the cherry tree? Good question. I have a book about that somewhere—" He disappeared between the shelves that towered around them like an enchanted forest of books.

Abraham Lincoln popped Walter into his hat, then Drew. The giggles in the hat grew louder. Each time he put a student inside, the hat grew taller and taller on his head—like Pinocchio's nose, only straight up.

"How does he do that?" said Norman, Nelson, and Neville Treble at the same time.

"He's a magician," said Marybeth in awe.

"It must be bigger on the inside than on the outside," said Katie, "like a spaceship or something."

"It's a *hat*," said Simon Snoot, rolling his eyes.

"Shh!" said Louie, bent over his lap with his fingers flying. "I'm almost to level seventy-two if I can just avoid getting eaten."

The hat gulped down Louie, leaving his video game beeping on the floor.

"Whoa," called Louie from inside the hat. "This is *cool*."

"Put me in!" the other students cried, clambering around Abraham Lincoln. "Put me in your hat!"

"No, don't go in the hat!" said Henry frantically. "*That's not Abraham Lincoln.*" He didn't care who heard him now. People were disappearing into his Art. This was not good.

"Stand back, you gelatinous filibuster!" Oscar waved his feather duster in Dragon-Lincoln's face, but Dragon-Lincoln only stuck out his tongue.

Jade stood up and faced the rest of the class with her hands on her hips. "Henry says stay away from the hat, and I think we should listen to Henry."

Henry stared at her.

So did the rest of the students. "But Simon says—" began Katie.

"Who ever listens to what *Simon* says?" said Jade. "Simon said there wasn't really a dragon in class, and there *was*. We all saw it. There was fire and smoke and roaring, and anyway, *who else* do you think sat on our art project? I say, if there's a *dragon*, then you'd better listen to a *knight*." She pointed a glittery finger at Henry and waited, expectantly. Henry, utterly flummoxed, raised his hand a little and waved.

Abraham Lincoln growled, picked up Jade by her suspenders, and flung her into his hat with the others. Then he straightened it on his head and smiled one of Miss Pimpernel's best Ha-Ha-Aren't-I-Funny smiles. The class erupted in laughter.

Henry stepped toward Dragon-Lincoln with his eraser held high. But there was something about the smiles on his classmates' faces that made him feel sorry. He had drawn this crooked-nosed, tall-hatted man, and laughed as he sat on the floor of his bedroom, imagining all of the things in the world that could hide in such a hat. He was always afraid people would laugh *at* his drawings. But now everyone was laughing *because* of his drawing, and that was different. That made him glow colors inside, as if a sunset was buried in his bones.

But he had to erase it. The drawing belonged on his door at home, not at school, not in front of the whole world. He had to save Oscar. He thought of Dennis Duckman, whose imagination had carried him away, never to be seen again.

But what if your imagination didn't carry *you* away—what if it carried away everyone else? The whole school might be in danger.

But even if he *could* tackle a nearly-seven-foot-tall president with a massive left hand and erase his greedy hat, what would happen to Trina, Walter, Drew, Louie, and Jade? If they were *inside* his drawing, would they disappear along with the drawing?

Then from deep within the hat came the sound of Jade's singing:

> *The phony foe was sly, and cunning too,*
> *But brave Sir Henry rose and roared, "Hey, you!*
> *Surrender, peddler of pernicious fire,*
> *Or poetry shall be your downfall dire!"*

Trumpets. Golden trumpets. There they were again, thrilling him to his fingertips. The day was still a story. The knight was still a hero.

"You heard her—*poetry shall be your downfall.* We have to defeat the dragon with poetry!" Henry said, though he had no idea what that meant. "Um . . . Roses are red. . . ," he said, but stopped. That was the wrong kind of poem.

"Dragons are green," added Katie helpfully.

"Your nose is the crookedest I've ever seen!" finished Oscar.

There was a pause. Dragon-Lincoln stuck his left thumb in his ear and wiggled his fingers at them.

"That was the dumbest poem I've ever heard," sneered Simon Snoot.

"No," mumbled Jade's voice, "Poetry shall be his DOWNFALL."

Downfall . . . downfall . . . What in the world was she talking about?

"I found it!" said Mr. Boolean, emerging from the bookshelf-forest. His face was lit up like the Fourth of July. "I found the answer. The incident of the cherry tree is about *George Washington*, but it didn't actually happen. The story isn't true. It's apocryphal!"

"Hey, that isn't very nice to say," said Oscar, who had called a nasty sixth grader *apocryphal* last week for stealing his lunch money.

"Mr. Boolean!" cried Henry, struck with a sudden idea. "Do you have a poetry book?"

"Do I have a poetry book? *Do I have a poetry book?* I

thought you would never ask." Mr. Boolean picked up a huge volume from the corner of his desk. "Why, this just came in the mail today—*The Oxford Book of Rhyme, Reason, and Versification*, complete with footnotes! My favorite poem is here on page 978: 'I too am not a bit tamed . . . I sound my barbaric YAWP over the roofs of the world . . .'"

Henry grabbed the book from Mr. Boolean's hands and threw it as hard as he could at Abraham Lincoln. Lincoln ducked, and the book made a perfect YAWP sound against the side of the hat, sending it tumbling to the floor. Downfall.

"Henry Penwhistle!" gasped the librarian. "I have never seen poetry so misused in my life! You should be ashamed of yourself."

Trina, Walter, Drew, Louie, and Jade all rolled out of the hat, laughing. Henry made a dive for the hat, eraser in hand, but Dragon-Lincoln got to it first. The man with the crooked nose pounced on the hat and slapped it back onto his head. He stomped and stamped and trampled on *The Oxford Book of Rhyme, Reason, and Versification*, then roared a very un-Lincolnish roar and stormed out of the library.

Henry recognized a temper tantrum when he saw it, and he knew what that meant. It meant the dragon wasn't afraid of him anymore. The dragon was *angry*. His Art was now his enemy.

This was no longer a chase. It was a battle.

"I'm sorry, Mr. Boolean," said Henry, pulling Oscar toward the door, "but we have to go."

"Wait!" said the librarian. "Don't you want to hear about George Washington? And where did Abraham Lincoln go?"

"Look! My octagon was here!" Oscar pointed to a poster of the solar system on the wall. The planets were gone. In their places were circular holes with little jagged teeth marks around the edges.

Just then Henry and Oscar felt a firm grip on their shoulders, and they turned their heads to find that the grip belonged to Principal Bunk. "Henry Penwhistle and Oscar Rockbottom, I think we should have a little talk."

CHAPTER 9
THE PRINCIPAL'S OFFICE

PRINCIPAL BUNK STEERED Henry and Oscar toward his office, which was right next to the school's main entrance. "You wait right here, Oscar," he said. "I'll talk to Henry first." Oscar sat down on the bench outside the office, giving Henry a sympathetic look as he did so, while the principal led Henry inside and shut the door.

"Can't Oscar come in too?" Henry didn't want to leave his friend alone for even a moment—not with a dragon-who-might-at-any-moment-turn-into-an-Oscar-eating-dinosaur roaming around the school.

"Have a seat, Henry." Henry sat on the brown leather sofa. The principal sat down at his desk. His glued-on smile was still on his face, but it didn't belong there. His eyes were not happy. He stared for a long time at Henry's aluminum foil armor and milk-carton helmet. On the floor beside his desk was a tower of textbooks that reached as tall as his head—math textbooks and spelling textbooks and grammar textbooks and science textbooks and history textbooks, like one of those huge pillars that hold up the ceilings of ancient buildings. At the very bottom, squashed under the weight of the tower, was a book that looked different, but Henry couldn't see what it was.

"That was not very funny," Principal Bunk said finally, "to tell a joke about a dragon right in front of the Bored Members. Do you want them to think we don't teach you properly at La Muncha? Do you want me to lose my job, Henry?"

"It wasn't a joke," mumbled Henry. But he thought, *If it wasn't funny, then why did you laugh?*

"And Miss Pimpernel informed me that while she was temporarily separated from her glasses this morning, someone *sat* on the class's Art Project. A beautiful box flattened. Twenty bunnies smashed into paper pulp. I was never sure this art show was a good idea. I'm still not sure."

Henry scrunched down lower on the sofa and gazed out the window behind the principal's head. A cloud that looked like a fire engine drove by. He swung his legs to make the clock tick faster. He couldn't stay there. He was a knight, and there was a dragon on the loose. He had to save the day.

Principal Bunk leaned forward in his chair. "How are you feeling, Henry?"

Now it was Henry's turn to stare. How was he feeling? He had wrestled an octopus this morning. He had just watched five of his classmates disappear into Abraham Lincoln's hat. He might be the cause of his best friend becoming dinosaur dinner. Was there even a *name* for that feeling?

"Henry, is there a dragon inside of you?" the principal continued. "Is there a little beast scratching against your heart, wanting to get out and be mean and angry at the world?"

"No, there's a dragon *outside* of me. *That's* the problem!" If only he could stuff the dragon back into his head, he could make it behave. He could teach it right and wrong. He could tell it about chivalry.

"Now, Henry, dragons just don't *happen* in real life. I

know Miss Pimpernel told you what a metaphor is. I think what you are calling a *dragon* is really just something inside of you that doesn't want to be happy."

This was the most ridiculous thing Henry had ever heard. Grown-ups were *crazy*. He had always suspected it, and here was proof. "But it's *not* a metaphor! I'm not saying something is something else when it isn't!" He swung his legs even faster. At this rate, he would never save the day. The dragon would scorch the day. The dragon would drown it. The dragon would smear it all over the sidewalk like stepped-on sunshine.

Then something slid across the window. It was a sticky, slimy, slippery Something. If you left a bowl of lime jello mixed with applesauce and smashed peas under your bed for a month, and then threw the blob of what was leftover against a window and watched it slide down the glass and leave a trail of blobby green blubber behind it, you would have an idea of what that Something looked like. Henry's stomach rolled over.

Principal Bunk straightened the intercom microphone on his desk and lined up his pens in a straight line. "Henry, we all get angry sometimes. We all have those days when we just want to break a few windows and stomp on flowers." He leaned back again, sighed a deep sigh, and straightened out the corners of his smile. "Do you know what *tame* means, Henry? It means *under control*. Think of it as the opposite of a lion—something safe enough to keep in your house and pet between the ears, like a kitten— or a bunny! *Imagination* is a wild animal, like an alligator, or a shark, or a polar bear. And do you know what the problem with wild animals is, Henry? They make messes! So *untidy*. So *unpredictable*. You must keep that imagina- tion of yours on a leash at all times." (Suddenly two eyes appeared in the sticky, slimy, slippery Something at the window, and they stared furiously at Principal Bunk.) "You must either tame the dragon inside you, or you must slay it!" The principal said this with such force that he brought his fists down heavily on the desk and stood up. But as he did so, his desk chair wobbled and fell into the tower of textbooks.

The tower toppled. Math and science and grammar and history cascaded like a waterfall of knowledge, leaving a mess of mixed-up numbers and words and wars and dis- coveries all over the carpet.

And there at the bottom of the pile, the book that looked different had been knocked open. It lay crookedly on the floor, its pages spread wide, and Henry could hardly believe his eyes. There were drawings, dozens and dozens of drawings, filling the open pages—and all the drawings were of a bright orange robot wearing boots and boxing gloves, soaring through space or juggling dinosaurs or stomping through forests of purple trees.

Quick as a frog's tongue, the principal snatched up the book and closed it. On the cover, Henry could see the scrawl of a name in a kid's loopy handwriting.

Cleaver Bunk

"That's a sketchbook just like mine!" Henry exclaimed. "Did you draw those pictures?"

"A long time ago," said the principal sharply. "You shouldn't have seen that. It's rubbish."

"If it's rubbish, then why did you keep it?"

Principal Bunk turned his chair upright again and sat down. He looked at the sketchbook he was holding and gently laid one hand on the front cover, as if it were a tiny animal and he were trying to feel its heartbeat. His glued-on smile was gone. Underneath it was the saddest mouth Henry had ever seen.

"I know it's fun to imagine things," the principal said quietly. "*I know.* But the world doesn't care about your art, Henry. The world will laugh and turn away. The world only cares about facts and numbers and budgets. I'm sorry, but it is my job to prepare you for the world you're going to have to live in, Henry: *the real world.*"

"What's his name?" Henry said.

The principal's forehead wrinkled. "Whose name?"

"The robot in your drawings."

Principal Bunk peered at Henry silently for several moments. His face grew pink with embarrassment. Then he whispered, "Mr. Stompawog Laserfist," and a little smile danced at the corner of his mouth—a smile that was not glued on, but was his very own.

Henry stared at him, astonished. The principal wasn't a supervillain at all. He was just a sad little boy who grew up.

"Now, Henry, I want you to tell me the truth," said Principal Bunk, shaking the little smile away and looking stern again. "Did *you* sit on the bunny box?"

At that moment the window cracked opened above the principal's head and the World's Slimiest Giant Slug

squished spectacularly into the office. No, it was the oppo-site of a squish. It was a squoosh. It was an unexpected, dramatically gooey, disgusting-slime-exploding-in-all-di-rections, whooshing SQUOOOOOSH! It left the window draped in a thick, sticky, gluey curtain that even the sharpest spike of a ferocious razor-tipped porcupine could not pen-etrate. And before Henry could say anything in warning, the slug burped its blubbery Something all over Principal Bunk, gluing him and his sketchbook to the chair of his desk. Then it squooshed out the door.

The principal stared at Henry in horror. His suit was slathered in slime. Slime was trickling down his cheeks and dripping off his chin onto the desk. His fingers were already sticking together as he tried to wipe the slime off his nose.

Henry leaped to his feet. "I'm sorry, Principal Bunk, but I have to go. I have to save the school." He turned toward the door, then hesitated and looked back at the principal again. "I like your robot." Then he ran after the giant slug-dragon, which squished and squashed and squooshed past Oscar and out into the main hallway. Henry saw that the glass doors leading out of the school were covered with a curtain of slime, just like the window in Principal Bunk's office. The slug winked naughtily at him. With one last burp, it turned itself inside out, reared its dragon head, lifted its dragon wings, and flew away down the hall.

Oscar gaped at the oozing greenish grossness all over his shoes. "What *is* this?"

"It's the World's Stickiest Slime," said Henry. "Jump or you'll be glued to the floor!"

Oscar jumped onto dry ground. He and Henry dashed after the dragon.

"JANITOR," crackled the principal's voice over the intercom. "JANITOR, COME TO MY OFFICE IMMEDIATELY ... AND BRING ... TISSUES ... "

Henry and Oscar did not have to run far. The dragon squeezed its scaly body through the door of the boys' bathroom. As soon as the boys ran through the door, they saw something long and green shimmy down one of the sink drains.

Oscar ran to the sink and leaned over it. "Okay, we know you're in there," he yelled down the drain before Henry could shush him. "So come out, you cockamamie bumbershoot!"

They felt the bathroom tremble around them. The pipes rattled. The sinks rocked and bumped against the walls. Henry wasn't sure he wanted to know what the dragon had turned into this time. But he did know that as soon as he got home, he was going to take a big fat permanent marker and write on the inside of his armor a very, very important rule of chivalry:

DON'T INSULT ANYTHING THAT HAS JUST SHIMMIED DOWN THE DRAIN.

"Uh oh," said Oscar.

"Plug it up!" Henry yelled. "Plug up the drain! No, wait—plug up *all* the drains." They grabbed handfuls of paper towels and stuffed them tightly into every sink drain. Then Oscar glanced towards the toilet stalls, and within a few seconds, every roll of toilet paper was unrolled, and there was no longer a single open pipe in the entire bathroom.

The boys were quiet for several minutes, and they listened.

The trembling and rattling and bumping ceased.

The air conditioning vent above their heads hummed.

One of the faucets drip-drip-dripped onto a soggy paper towel.

"I think it's gone," whispered Oscar.

"Shhh," said Henry.

They stood perfectly still for a long time, as the clock on the wall counted out the silence.

So that was that. The dragon—his Work of Art—was gone. Down the drain and gone forever.

A surge of relief flooded Henry's chest, and then, suddenly, a different feeling. He turned away so Oscar couldn't see his face. For the first time that day, Henry began to be afraid that he might cry.

CHAPTER 10

A WORLD WITHOUT DRAGONS

HENRY STARED glumly at the worksheet in front of him. Fractions. He hated fractions.

$$\frac{2}{6} + \frac{4}{6}$$

All he could see was an elephant's trunk and a pair of dancing legs balancing on top of two yo-yos. They just needed a clown or two and they'd have a circus.

$$\frac{2}{6} + \frac{4}{6} = \frac{1}{8}$$

There you go, he thought. *A tightrope walker on a tightrope with a clown underneath.* But he knew that wasn't right. How was he supposed to do math when clowns and elephants kept

114

getting in the way?

"Now, Henry, I know you can do this problem," said Miss Pimpernel, leaning over his desk. He didn't have to look up to know that she was wearing her I-Have-More-Patience-Than-a-Snail-in-a-Traffic-Jam smile. "The bottoms are the same, so all you have to do is add the tops. What's four plus two?"

"Orange," he mumbled.

"I'm sorry, I didn't hear you."

"ORANGE."

"Henry, four plus two is not orange. Four and two are numbers, and orange is a color."

"It's the same thing," he whispered, low enough for Miss Pimpernel not to hear as she moved on to help another student. Across the room, he could hear Simon Snoot snickering, and his cheeks burned.

Henry glanced around the classroom. The lights seemed dimmer than they had been before. The colors seemed different. The reds and yellows and purples had all run away. The desks looked like they never even thought about kicking their legs or clicking their heels together. This was the real world. A world where pictures never pop out of places they aren't supposed to. A world of fractions and spelling tests and doorknobs. A world without dragons.

Miss Pimpernel's class was antsy after the excitement of the morning, and the students kept glancing at Henry as if, at any moment, he might pull something terrifying or magical out of his backpack. *But they don't know*, Henry thought. *They don't know that it's all over.* Out of the corner of his eye he saw Jade passing a note to Louie, who, Henry noticed, was not playing his video game anymore. Jade saw Henry looking at her and smiled.

He quickly turned back to his worksheet and stared at the numbers again. Pulling some colored markers out of his desk, he drew eyes and a nose and a mouth on the clownish 8, and covered its head with kinky red hair. He gave the dancing 4 a body and a tall black hat. The wavy elephant trunk of the 2 grew longer and longer under his pencil, and a great wrinkly elephant began to fill his paper and shoot purple peanuts out of his nose.

Beside him, Oscar was busily scribbling numbers all over his own worksheet. The *right* numbers, Henry knew. Oscar was a scientist. Scientists understand math. In the future, if Henry ever needed to know math, he would call Oscar, and Oscar would tell him the answer.

And Oscar would never know that once, on a strange day at La Muncha Elementary School, he had almost been eaten by a dinosaur.

Henry felt so small that even his armor seemed too big for him all of a sudden. He lifted the bottom corner of his raincoat to find some chivalry that would make him feel better, but the marker there had smudged, and all he could read was

Why did he need his armor, anyway? There was no more dragon. Maybe there never was one. Maybe he had made it all up after all. Like the time during recess when he imagined the swinging tire was a flying shark and he fought it so hard with his sword that it actually began to *look* like a flying shark. It was only after Miss Pimpernel had pulled him away and he realized the rest of the kids on the playground were all staring at him that the shark began to look like a tire swing again.

"HENRY, WHAT ARE YOU DOING?" The shark

memory vanished. Miss Pimpernel was standing over him, her hands on her hips. A dozen of her less-happy smiles fought for a spot on her face. Henry hadn't even thought about what he was doing, until he looked down and saw it. When he had reached the edge of the worksheet, he had forgotten to stop drawing. The purple peanuts shooting from the elephant's nose spiraled all the way across his desk and finally exploded into fireworks on the pages of his math textbook.

Oops.

"Henry," sighed Miss Pimpernel, shaking her head. "A little imagination now and then is nice, but when it flies off a piece of paper and invades the rest of the world, it has gone too far."

Too far. His whole day had gone too far. He looked up at her quivering cheeks and her beaver-teeth hair shining under the fluorescent lights overhead. He wanted to say: *Miss Pimpernel, remember, remember. What was your superpower? Did you ever rescue a mermaid from a three-headed sea monster by punching it with your Incredible Fist of Ice? Did you turn invisible every Thursday and make silly faces at the people who couldn't see you? Did you sing so loudly that your music could crack the Walls of*

Despair in which the Saddest Smile was imprisoned? Did you have a cape that swirled behind you in the wind, and did you fly over the moon and back? Why did you forget?

But what came out of his mouth was this: "I don't have It, do I?"

"You don't have what?"

"Whatever you don't have. The reason you won't draw."

"Henry, what on earth are you talking about?"

The words came tumbling out of him now. "I don't like fractions."

"Yes, I can see that."

"I like drawing."

"I know you do, but—"

"I like dragons."

"But, Henry—"

"I'm glad the bunny box got smashed."

He knew at once that he had gone too far—again. The rest of the students in the class dropped their pencils and stared at him, then at their teacher. Miss Pimpernel stiffened and stood up straight. "Well," she said, and the word came out sounding squished and smothered. "I like bunnies." Her smiles were gone. Every single one of them.

The I-Have-More-Patience-Than-a-Snail-in-a-Traffic-Jam smile had been run over by a semitruck. The I-Knew-You-Could-Do-It smile had decided you couldn't. The Look-at-Me-I'm-the-Queen-of-Elementary-School smile had fled the throne. And suddenly, Henry would have drawn all of the bunnies in the world to bring those smiles back.

But that day, there was to be no more drawing of bunnies in Miss Pimpernel's classroom. For at that moment, a puddle of water spread under the door and soaked her shoes. "What in the world?" She walked over to the classroom door. Henry could hear a faint rumbling and gurgling coming from the hallway, growing louder. And louder. He looked at Oscar, who had heard it too.

Henry felt again as he had felt that morning when he looked at the blank, empty door of his bedroom. He adjusted the helmet on his head. He straightened the collar of his armor. He picked up his backpack and strapped it to his back. "Be brave, Sir Henry," he whispered as Miss Pimpernel's hand closed on the doorknob.

Years later, when Henry Penwhistle remembered this day and told the story again and again to himself, it seemed to him that this was the moment—the hand on the door-knob moment—when everything changed. Before, the adventure with the dragon was like a balloon bobbing at the end of a string in Henry's hand, trying to break out of his grasp. After this moment, the string came loose, and Henry realized he had never known—indeed, no one at La Muncha Elementary School had ever known—just how wildly an imagination can fly when it has broken free.

Perhaps the Bored Members were wise to take away doorknobs. For it is a dangerous thing to open a door.

"Miss Pimpernel!" said Oscar, jumping out of his seat. "I don't think you should—"

But she did.

CHAPTER 11
THE GREEN SHIP

AS SOON AS MISS PIMPERNEL opened the door, a wave of water knocked her over, swelled into the classroom, and plastered the door against the wall.

The students scrambled onto their desks to avoid the flood. Henry looked towards the hallway, and at first he thought the roof had blasted off and a rainstorm had begun over the school. But then he saw the smoke rings of the dragon's fiery breath as it swept down the hall, setting off the emergency sprinklers on the ceiling. The walls of the school shook with an unmistakably dragonish roar.

Henry wanted to jump and cheer and skip and sing.

And then he wanted to throw up.

Happiness and fear tangled themselves up in his stomach.

The principal's voice crackled over the intercom: "ATTENTION, STUDENTS AND TEACHERS. WE SEEM TO HAVE A VERY MINOR PLUMBING PROBLEM. PLEASE PROCEED CAREFULLY OUT THE DOORS TO THE PLAYGROUND. DO NOT PANIC. DO NOT SCREAM. DO NOT RUN. AND IF YOU NEED TO USE THE BATHROOM, PLEASE TRY TO HOLD IT IN."

Unfortunately, no one could hold in the bathrooms.

"The bathrooms are exploding! The bathrooms are explooooooooddddiiiiiinnggg!" shrieked the kindergartners. They were floating down the hallway on their snack trays, clinging to them like little boats, as chocolate milk cartons and carrot sticks flew left and right. Teachers opened the doors of their classrooms to lead their classes outside to the playground, and the river swept into the rooms, gathered up desks and chairs and pupils in its soggy arms, and swept out again.

Then something happened that Henry would never forget. Miss Pimpernel pulled herself up onto her desk, straightened her hair that glistened with water, and held her arms out to her students. "No need to be afraid," she said calmly. "It's just a little plumbing problem. These things happen. Now I want you to grab each other's hands and hold on." And then— oh then—she took hold of the long bulletin board behind her desk, and with a strength none knew she possessed, she wrenched it off the wall and threw it into the middle of the classroom with a mighty splash, where it bobbed like a raft. If she had been wearing a cape, it wouldn't have been any more impressive.

"It's made of cork! It'll float!" Oscar said.

"Everyone get on!" Miss Pimpernel said. The students jumped off their desks and began to pull themselves onto the corkboard raft.

The principal's voice crackled above them for a second time: "ATTENTION, STUDENTS AND TEACHERS. SOMEONE APPEARS TO HAVE SEALED ALL THE DOORS OF THE SCHOOL WITH SLIMY GREEN GLUE. PLEASE CLIMB CAREFULLY OUT THE WINDOWS."

Then a few seconds later: "NEVER MIND. THE WINDOWS DON'T SEEM TO BE OPENING EITHER. WELL, A LITTLE WATER NEVER HURT

ANYONE. IN FACT, I SUGGEST WE ALL TURN THIS INTO A TEACHABLE MOMENT. THERE ARE MANY *WATER* WORDS HIGHLY SUITABLE FOR SPELLING TESTS. *AQUAMARINE*, FOR INSTANCE. *ANTEDILUVIAN. BEDRAGGLED.* SO JUST SIT TIGHT, FOLKS, AND KEEP LEARNING!" The intercom sputtered with static as the voice continued, more distant, "Speaking of sitting tight, will someone— get me—out—of—this—CHAIR!"

So Principal Bunk was still stuck. And so were the windows and doors. *The dragon glued us inside the school. It glued us with super-sticky slug slime. Why would it do that?* wondered Henry as he clung to the edge of the raft. He struggled to get on as it was swept out the door of the classroom and into the hallway. Jade grabbed his arm to keep him from floating away. Oscar, still in the water, clung to Henry's backpack. The rising water gurgled by, and with it a rising tide of waterlogged backpacks and textbooks and math homework. The hallway had become a rushing river flowing around the great circle of the school, and around, and around, and around.

Miss Pimpernel sat tall and straight on the raft like a

queen, like a president, like a genie, like a superhero, and oh, she was magnificent. Henry could tell from her bewildered face that she had no idea what to make of all this. But she was not going to let that stop her from teaching her class. "Now that we're all settled, let's have our spelling test. Jade, spell *danger*."

Jade looked over Henry's head, at something behind them all, and sang out loudly:

> *Danger, spelled D-R-A-G-O-N,*
> *Did smite them with a chilly fear, but THEN*
> *Across the smitten sea a ship shape shone*
> *And in dank darkness groaned a ghastly groan*
> *As Henry, pure of heart o'er all the realm,*
> *Put on his chivalry and took the helm.*

There were the golden words again, blazing across his quest. His quest! There was still a quest! But Henry felt the sharp pinch of guilt in his heart. He was not full of chivalry and pure of heart. In his sketchbook was a picture of a dinosaur that proved he was not.

Then Jade leaned over and whispered, "Good luck," and—pushed him off the raft.

"Hey!" he yelled, and gulped a mouthful of water.

"Hey!" sputtered Oscar, grabbing Henry even more tightly around the waist as they both bobbed under the whirling water. Henry coughed and kicked and managed to turn over onto his back. And that's when he saw what Jade had seen coming around the curve of the hallway. It was a ship—long and sleek and slightly green. He blinked once, and saw a white sail billowing out, though there was no wind, of course. He blinked twice, and the sail looked like a huge bat's wing with a single claw at the very tip scratching a trail in the ceiling as it went by. The prow of the ship hung out hungrily over the water and slurped up the kindergartners' carrots.

"There it is!" yelled Henry. He grabbed the ship's stern as it passed by, and it felt sharp and scaly like a dragon's tail—for that's what it was. He and Oscar scrambled aboard.

The dragon-ship did not appreciate having passengers. It arched and twisted. A claw reached out from underneath, but Henry and Oscar stayed close together and held on tight. The dragon couldn't reach that far around onto its own back.

Henry squeezed his hand into his backpack and pulled

out two black eyepatches. He gave one to Oscar.

"Avast, ye scallawag!" Henry called in his most Long-John-Silver-y voice.

Oscar put on the eyepatch. "Yo-ho-ho, ye scurvy dog!"

"We buccaneers be commandeerin' this ship!"

"Arrrrrrr!"

Henry reached back into his backpack for the eraser, but at that moment the dragon-ship lurched to the right, and he had to hold on with both hands or he would

slip right off into the water again. A sign above a door up ahead said CAFETERIA, and the dragon-ship was aiming directly at it.

The cafeteria door was wide and had a window in the top half of it. CRACK! The glass shattered inward. The front of the ship changed back into a dragon's head. Its teeth bit down on the edge of the glass-less window. The ship became a dragon's body once again, and it squeezed and wiggled through the hole. Henry and Oscar were pushed further and further backwards and had to grasp tightly onto the end of the tail, or the water would sweep them down the hallway.

And then they, too, were pulled through the hole by the dragon's tail. They landed on dry floor on the other side. They were in a little hallway filled with stacks of cafeteria trays and little compartments holding forks and spoons and napkins.

The little hallway opened into the cafeteria, the circular room at the center of the circular school—the hole in the donut. Its heavy door had kept out the water so far (with the help of a lot of dishrags stuffed into the cracks around the edges). Luckily, the Lunch Lady had not opened it to see what was happening in the main hallway.

Henry and Oscar heard her scream even before they saw her. They ran into the cafeteria just as the Lunch Lady turned around and found herself face-to-face with a dragon.

Stretched across the cafeteria above her head was a banner that said NATIONAL VEGETABLE WEEK. Plastic vegetables hung from the ceiling, along with the other classes' Art Projects. Drawings of eggplants papered the walls.

The Lunch Lady's face was the color of peaches. There was a smudge of tomato sauce on her chin. The dripping wet curls on her forehead were the color of scrambled eggs. She stood still and silent with her mouth wide open, as if the scream had fallen out and she was too surprised to pick it up again and keep on screaming.

The dragon stared back at the Lunch Lady as if she were the fairest damsel it had ever seen. (Or as if she were lunch. Henry couldn't quite tell which.) Then it stretched out a long green tongue and licked the Lunch Lady on the nose.

"I beg your pardon!" said the Lunch Lady. "I do not kiss dragons, no matter how handsome they think they are." And she popped the dragon on the snout with the frying pan.

The dragon howled in pain.

Henry expected it to charge at her, or send a ball of fiery breath rolling across the room. He did not expect it to spread its wings, lunge into the air, grab hold of a dangling cauliflower, and—

hang there.

After the thunder of the flood and the crashing of the ship against walls and waves and floating desks, the silence now sounded like the stab of a period at the end of a long sentence. The dragon swayed gently, suspended from the ceiling, out of reach of Henry and Oscar. On one side of it was the first grade's sculpture of a farmer made of popsicle sticks and candy wrappers. On the other side of it was the fifth grade's papier-mâché broccoli bouquet tied with multicolored ribbons.

Henry remembered Abraham Lincoln in the library hissing, "Can *sssssssomeone pleasssssse ssssshow me where the cafeteria isssssss?*" The dragon had finally found the cafeteria. And now it was exactly where it wanted to be—hanging in the National Vegetable Week art show, waiting to be greatly admired and applauded by one and all.

CHAPTER 12

DAMSEL IN DISTRESS, DAMSEL TO THE RESCUE

HENRY GAZED at his Work of Art, dangling there for all the world to see. *Maybe it can just stay there*, he thought. Maybe no one would notice there was a dragon hanging with the vegetable art. Or maybe everyone would. Maybe they would say, "That looks like just the sort of awesome thing Henry Penwhistle would draw," and he would hear them say it but pretend as if he hadn't heard, and then he would spend the rest of the day with a dragon-sized smile inside his heart.

The dragon's eyes searched out Henry far below, and they seemed to say, "Look! Look at me! Aren't I marvelous? Please tell me I am marvelous."

You are, thought Henry. *You're absolutely marvelous.*

The Lunch Lady stomped over to Henry and Oscar, still holding her frying pan. "Young men, *what* is a dragon doing in my cafeteria, and *why* does it smell like wet chalk?"

It suddenly dawned on Henry that the Lunch Lady, unlike Miss Pimpernel and Principal Bunk, was paying attention. Closely. She not only *saw* the dragon, she even *smelled* it. "I—I drew it," Henry stammered. "With chalk. Mostly."

"*You* drew it?" she said, sounding almost impressed. She turned around and considered the dragon slowly, from the fearsome claws on its feet to its silver-dagger teeth. The dragon stretched its wings as wide as they would stretch. It looked as thoughtful and tragic as a Greek statue—a statue hanging from a cauliflower.

"You have a fascinating style—a style of your very own," the Lunch Lady said finally, as if she were declaring the ripeness of a tomato. The dragon puffed a perfect circle of smoke out of the corner of its mouth. "I have never seen a dragon quite like it. *Unique.* So many shapes! I can almost see the shapes moving around—inside of the dragon and out-side of the dragon—as if it wanted to be other things too.

The face is a bit crooked—" The dragon's jaws twitched.

"He always draws crooked faces!" said Oscar.

Henry felt his own face grow warm. Not because of the crooked faces, but because she had said his drawing was *fascinating*. She was talking to him like she would talk to a grown-up artist.

"Crooked faces might just be one of the things that make your art *yours* and nobody else's," the Lunch Lady said, drawing closer to the dragon and inspecting its scales. The dragon thrust its chest out proudly. "It might be the very thing that makes you famous someday. Yes. Nice work. Ask your parents to take you to an art museum sometime. Look for paintings by *Pablo Picasso* and *Wassily Kandinsky*. Funny names, aren't they? You'll like them. All wild shapes and colors."

Henry and Oscar stared at the Lunch Lady. They had never heard her say anything other than, "Would you like meatloaf or macaroni?" She frowned. "You kids think all I do is cook *lunch*. Here I am holding an *art show*, trying to bring some *culture* to this school, some *creativity*, some *joie de vivre*—"

"What's a zwadaveever?" whispered Henry.

"It's a kind of pickle," said Oscar, though Henry could tell he had no idea.

"—and all I get in return is a demand for a pizza party. *Pizza!* Pizza is not even a vegetable, and it's *National Vegetable Week*. It's enough to make an artist weep!" She wiped away a tear. "And that, I am sorry to say, is also the problem with this dragon." A whine erupted from the hanging dragon's throat, and Henry felt a groan in his own stomach. "It is not National *Dragon* Week," said the Lunch Lady firmly. "When I have a National Dragon Week art show, I will allow your excellent dragon to enter. But I doubt that will ever happen. It has taken me three years to convince Principal Bunk that an art show is a useful educational activity at all! I'm sorry, Henry, but I'm afraid this dragon is *not* a vegetable, shows no evidence of having *eaten* any vegetables, and in fact has absolutely *nothing to do* with vegetables. I have no choice but to disqualify it from the National Vegetable Week art show."

The dragon dropped to the floor with a mighty *thump*. It let out a terrible wail that rolled on and on, as if a splinter of lightning had broken the heart of a thundercloud. Then it wrapped the Lunch Lady tightly in its wings until all you could see of her was her scrambled-egg-colored hair.

"Unhand me!" mumbled the Lunch Lady from inside the dragon's wings.

But the dragon did not unhand her. Swinging its tail from side to side, it batted at the lunch tables, turning them topsy-turvy and shoving them into the corner of the cafeteria. The noise was thunderous. Henry and Oscar had to duck to avoid getting hit by flying chairs. With a clattering and scraping of metal and wood, the dragon piled the tables into a triangle-shaped fortress, like a tepee. Then it placed the Lunch Lady inside, beat its tail against one last table to close the gap, and roared again.

"Stop!" yelled Henry at the top of his voice.

The dragon turned and looked at him. Across its face danced the pictures Henry recognized so well, the pictures that had danced their ghostly chalk dance on his bedroom door. The three-headed gorilla with banana-detecting antennae. The Puffleburpachoo with its Very Unusual Tooth. The dinosaur—

No!

"You don't belong here," Henry said resolutely. "You don't fit in here. You might turn into—" But he couldn't say it in front of Oscar. "You might *hurt* someone." He took his backpack off his back and dumped the contents onto the floor. Then he held the backpack out, open, towards the dragon. "Come on. *Please.* Get into my backpack and we'll go home and this will all be over, and we'll have so many adventures, just the two of us! We can have swordfights and piggyback rides and races and burping contests, and we can go on quests to find lost socks and ogres' toothbrushes, and I can teach you how to roast marshmallows with your breath and make s'mores. We can do anything you want if you'll just *go back to my bedroom!*"

The dragon's eyes narrowed. It looked up at the hanging art projects, rose into the air, and grabbed the cauliflower with its teeth again, hanging on desperately. Principal Bunk's sad voice floated back into Henry's mind, and he shouted at the dragon, "The world doesn't care about you. The world will laugh at you. The world only cares about facts and numbers and budgets." The cauliflower's string broke, and the dragon tumbled to the floor. *But that's not true,* Henry thought suddenly. *Oscar cares. My parents care. The bus driver cares.* He remembered Jade's poetry echoing in his chest and her glittery finger pointing at him in the library. *Jade cares.*

"I don't want to have to erase you," he whispered. "Please don't make me have to erase you."

The dragon sniffed a mighty sniff, and all the eggplant drawings flew off the walls and stuck to its snout. It pulled them off one by one and swallowed them.

Henry stepped closer, holding out his backpack again, pleading. "You just have to turn into something smaller so you can get into my backpack. You could be a three-headed toad! Three-headed toads are awesome. Or a space chicken. Or an iguana."

"Or a wooly mammoth!" said Oscar.

"No," Henry hissed, "that's too big."

The papier-mâché broccoli bouquet disappeared down the dragon's throat. Three play dough pumpkins soon followed. The dragon began stomping towards a cornucopia of cardboard. "It's going to eat the whole art show! What are we going to do?" whispered Oscar.

Henry's shoulders slumped. He had tried, but the dragon wouldn't listen. "I'll erase it a little bit at a time," he said, "until it's so small it can fit in my backpack." Then he raised his eraser and yelled, "Henry forth!"

"Oscar forth!"

They ran toward the dragon with eraser and feather duster outstretched. The dragon's head swung around, and its nostrils steamed. Oscar held the handle of the feather duster between his two hands and twirled it furiously. "Take that, you Humuhumunukunukuapuaa!"

A cloud of dust danced around the dragon's head. Its nostrils twitched. Its eyes watered. Its mouth opened wider—and wider—and wider— "AAAAAAAAA . . . "

Henry reached inside and erased its teeth.

" . . . CHOOOO!" said the dragon. And immediately, its scaly green face glowed red with anger—or with shame. It gnashed its bare gums. It rolled its tongue around its mouth where its teeth should be, searching for them everywhere. And at last, realizing the great tragedy and indignity that had just occurred, it roared, swung its tail, and knocked over a table, sending it tumbling towards Henry and Oscar. They rolled out of the way and ducked behind another table.

Henry yelled his most lung-tickling Tarzan yell. Then he climbed up on the serving counter and leaped to grab hold of the nearest plastic carrot hanging from the ceiling.

"Here we go again," sighed Oscar.

The wind *whooooshed* around Henry's ears as he flew through the air. He swung from carrot to carrot, from carrot to broccoli, from broccoli to eggplant . . . until he was standing on the top of the fortress of tables the dragon had built around the Lunch Lady.

"Help! You've got to help me!" cried the Lunch Lady.

"I know, we're going to save you," yelled Oscar.

"No, no, I mean you've got to help me prepare for the party. Do you know how many people are going to be in this cafeteria for the art show today? Do you know how many pizzas I have to cook? How will they get cooked if I am stuck in here? Principal Bunk will fire me for sure! I'll have to go back to making bacon-grease biscuits at Waffle Heaven!"

"Oscar can do it!" said Henry. "He's good at counting pepperoni."

Oscar's face looked like a melted meatball. His eye patch had slid down to his ear. "I don't want to *cook*. Why do I have to make the pizzas when you get to be Tarzan?"

"I'm only saving the art show, but you're saving the whole school from having no lunch," said Henry. "So your chivalry is much bigger than mine." That was *kind of* telling the truth, wasn't it? But the underneath-truth was that he wanted Oscar to be as far away from the dragon as possible. As soon it decided to change shapes again, it could turn into the dinosaur.

"But you *always* get to be Tarzan, and I—"

"Oh, thank you, Oscar!" said the Lunch Lady. "Now in the refrigerator you'll find twenty-five big round pizza crusts . . ."

Oscar sighed and ran into the kitchen. He began slinging round crusts onto the counter. Henry grabbed hold of a long, stringy asparagus and swung with such spectacular swishy-ness that he could practically hear the monkeys of the jungle clapping in applause. The dragon swung out its left foreclaw to swipe at Henry, but Henry's eraser got to it first. Now the dragon was missing its right foreclaw *and* its left one. It sputtered a fiery spurt of indignation.

The asparagus broke loose from the ceiling, and Henry landed on a cart filled with trays of dirty dishes. The cart rolled right into the kitchen and rammed into the pantry shelves, and he ended up coughing in a cloud of flour.

He heard a crunch behind him. Oscar's octagon was crouched comfortably on the bottom shelf, minding its own business. It was eating its way through the cookies, the donuts, the plastic lids, the mixing bowls, and the pizza cutters. It had grown to several times its normal size.

"Hey!" Henry yelled. "I found your octagon!"

Oscar gasped in relief and peered in. "I think I'm going to need a bigger shoebox," he said.

Before Henry could answer, he heard the loud, impatient tapping of a foot.

He and Oscar peeked over the top of the serving counter.

The dragon was gone. In the middle of the cafeteria stood a big pair of cowboy boots with bright green spurs on the heels and chalky swirls of purple and yellow and orange all over the green leather—swirls that Henry had drawn while singing cowboy songs like "Home on the Range" at the top of his lungs in his room. One of the boots stomped on the floor, kicking up clouds of dust and sandwich crumbs. The cafeteria lights burned down like a Texas sun. In the distance, a police siren wailed like a coyote.

Henry crawled over to the pile on the floor where he had dumped out his backpack. He laid down his helmet and put on his cowboy hat. He tied a bandana around his neck. He hung his lasso around his arm, grabbed a banana from the serving counter, and stepped out into the open. "Get over here, you long-legged . . . two-toed . . . uh . . ."

"Granivorous Grinch!" yelled Oscar from the kitchen.

"Don't forget the cheese, Oscar!" yelled the Lunch Lady from the table fortress.

Henry twirled the banana around his finger. "Get over here, you long-legged two-toed Grinchy Graniverunch," he drawled. "This school ain't big enough for the both of us."

The boots charged at him. Henry stuck the banana in his pocket. He swung the lasso around three times and let it fly. "YEEEEEEHAAAAAAAW!" But one boot ran to the right, and the other boot ran to the left, and the lasso fell uselessly in between. The boots came back together and landed on top of Henry before he had time to switch from the lasso to the eraser. They kicked and stomped and tickled him with their spurs until he was forced to curl into a ball and cover his head, swinging his banana blindly in defense.

Behold! Sir Henry fights with mighty fruit
The foulest knave that ever wore a boot!

Jade strolled into the cafeteria from the hallway. Her hair was soaking wet, and her fuzzy scarf was soaking wet, and her suspenders were soaking wet, and she looked like she would be perfectly happy if she woke up soaking wet every day of her life. She put her hands on her hips and stared down at Henry. "Howdy, Pardner." The boots let Henry go and stood several feet away, tapping their toes, quite pleased with themselves.

This was like one of those nightmares when you walk out of your house and down the street thinking you're wearing a knight's shiny suit of armor and then suddenly you realize you're really wearing pink princess pajamas and then you realize everyone in the whole school is staring at you and you want to sink through the sidewalk all the way to China.

He was relieved to see her. But why couldn't she have walked in when he was swinging like Tarzan, or reaching bravely into the dragon's mouth to erase its teeth?

"Yeehaw," he whispered.

"Throw me the eraser," she said.

"What?"

"Throw me the eraser!" She kicked the toe of the left boot hard and ran the other direction. The boots galloped after her. Boy, could she run.

It took Henry several seconds to realize what she was

trying to do. He tossed the eraser. She caught it nimbly, laughing and dodging the boots the way he had seen soccer players dodging each other's feet in a game. And then he swung his lasso, letting it swoop and circle above his head. The loop of rope flew—

it fell—

it tightened around the left boot.

"Get 'em, Henry!" yelled Oscar from the kitchen. "Get that lazy, lame-duck—

"Have you put the pepperoni on yet?" called the Lunch Lady.

"—*lollygagging lagomorph.*"

"Oscar! I have an art show to host, and meanwhile I am being held captive by a dragon. That's hardly *lollygagging*! Nor do I resemble a *rabbit,* and it is quite insulting of you to say so."

"No, no, I'm sorry, I didn't mean you!" Oscar grabbed heaping handfuls of pepperoni and dumped them onto the pizzas.

Henry pulled one way. The boot pulled the other. The rope held fast. Jade circled back toward them, reaching out with the eraser. With a graceful sweep of her arm, she rubbed the boot into the great blue yonder.

The other boot skidded to a stop and hopped away in the other direction. Quick as a wink Henry lassoed it too, but the boot galloped so fast the rope flew out of his hands and bounced after the boot as it hopped into the kitchen.

Oscar's voice burst from behind the counter. "Come here, quick! I've got the boot! I'm sitting on it!—Whoooooooaaaaaaa, Nellie."

The boot began to grow.

Henry's heart sank to his toes. "NO!"

CHAPTER 13
A VORPAL BLADE

OSCAR HELD ON tightly as the bulging boot lifted him higher and higher off the floor and began to look less and less like a boot. The lasso was tightened around the neck of a fearsome head with a stubby green horn, and behind that was a huge body with two rows of diamond-shaped plates running down its back and tail. Two wide, bony, webbed wings like the wings of a bat opened outward and swept the creature—and Oscar—into the air.

"Is this supposed to be a *Stegosaurus*?" cried Oscar, clinging to one of the plates. "A *Stegosaurus* doesn't have wings. Why can't you ever get dinosaurs right? I can't believe you call yourself my friend and you drew a *Stegosaurus* wrong!"

There are worse reasons not to call me a friend, thought Henry, and his stomach felt like it was falling down a steep roller coaster after having eaten way too many cupcakes. For this was his dreaded picture, his worst-friend moment, his angry art come to life. And oh, how he wished he could stuff it back into his head, deep, deep down, where it would never find its way out again.

The sight of the *Stegosaurus* roaring above their heads, looking so much bigger than it had ever seemed on his bedroom door, brought the Big Fight back into his mind in an instant. He had drawn a *Tyrannosaurus rex*, just to please Oscar. Oscar had been working on his Lego laboratory so intently that he didn't even notice the picture that towered over them both until Henry tapped his foot and coughed. He remembered how proud he had been, how his stomach had tingled in anticipation of Oscar's happiness. Oscar, who had been trying so hard to find a *T. rex* skeleton in his basement.

Oscar had turned, stared at the drawing for a moment, and said, "What is *that* supposed to be?"

The tingling in Henry's stomach froze. "It's a *Tyrannosaurus rex*."

And then Oscar laughed.

He *laughed*. Henry's best friend in the whole world *laughed*.

"It has *ears*! *T. rexes* don't have long ears like that. It looks like a kangaroo!"

"Those are horns!" retorted Henry.

"They don't have long horns like that either," Oscar giggled. And then he rolled on the floor snorting and heaving and holding his stomach to keep the laughter from spilling out all over the carpet. "It's a *Kangahornus rex*!"

Henry felt small. He felt as puny as a peanut crushed in the teeth of a circus elephant.

His Art was a silly scribble after all.

And so began the pig-blobfish-skunk-trout-snouted-putrefied-armadillo-face war, and the crashing of the Lego laboratory, and the smearing of the finger paint, and the drawing of the angry picture that had led to this moment: Oscar on a winged *Stegosaurus* flying around the school cafeteria, with Henry standing helpless below.

He ran to grab the end of the lasso. Jade jumped onto the *Stegosaurus's* tail. Boy, could she jump. "Take that, ye villain with the monstrous breath!" Jade said. She erased the tail and fell to the floor again.

"Oscar, you're going to have to erase the wings," Henry yelled. Jade threw the eraser up to Oscar. Boy, could she throw.

"A *Stegosaurus* isn't supposed to *have* wings. Don't you ever pay attention to me at all? I pay attention to you. I memorized all the Knights of the Round Table because of you. And you go and draw a *Stegosaurus* with *wings*."

"I'm sorry!" *You have no idea how sorry I am*, thought Henry.

He had erased the dragon's teeth. That was a relief. But those terrible toothless dinosaur gums could still mash up Oscar into boy-flavored applesauce.

"Oscar, jump off!" Henry yelled.

"Look at me!" said Oscar. And Henry did look until his eyes burned with looking, for Oscar was a shining thing there on the back of that dinosaur, a flying shining knightly thing. His untucked shirt flapped wildly, and his shoelaces looked like the tails of a kite on a windy day. His mop of hair was so plastered to his face that all you could see was his chin—and that chin was held so high and proud that if he'd had a beard, it would have danced upon the ceiling.

For one brief moment, Henry wished *he* were the one up there shining like a hero, instead of Oscar.

"I'm Sir Oscar! I'm just as strong and brave as you are. I can fight the dinosaur."

"NO!" said Henry.

"Why NOT?"

But Henry couldn't tell him why not. He couldn't say, *Because I know how this adventure ends—I drew it, and your face will turn white with fear just before you are eaten.* Instead, he yelled, "Because I've got to save you!"

"But I want to do the saving this time!" said Oscar. "I want to be a knight!"

The dinosaur whirled above their heads, slamming into the plastic food and the art projects until the NATIONAL VEGETABLE WEEK banner was a limp necklace around its bony neck. Henry caught the end of the rope and felt himself jerked into the air. Jade grabbed his feet and tried as hard as she could to pull him down again. Chewed-up bits of plastic radishes and squash and onions rained down around them.

Oscar's voice was as broken as the radishes. "I just don't understand why you—"

"ERASE THE WINGS!" yelled Henry and Jade together.

Oscar swung the eraser, and the *Stegosaurus* tumbled, wingless, onto the cafeteria floor with a mighty thump. Oscar grabbed for a hanging eggplant, but missed. The dinosaur rolled over onto its side and stretched its scaly neck upward and opened its toothless jaws wide, and—

—the flying shining knightly boy fell in.

The dinosaur gulped, and there was no more Oscar.

Jade whispered, "It *ate him!*" but then she stood still and breathless as if a dragon's claws had tightened around her throat. Even her poetry was silent.

It's my fault, cried Henry on the inside, but no sound would come out of his mouth.

"I know—you can erase a hole in the stomach so Oscar can—" But Jade trailed off, realizing, as Henry did, that Oscar had been holding the eraser. It was gone.

"Henry! Oscar! What's happened?" called the Lunch Lady from her fortress. "What was all that racket? Has Oscar put the pizzas in the oven yet? It's almost lunchtime! The art show will be starting soon!"

Henry didn't answer.

There was no more Oscar.

Someone had cut a hole in the world. There was a blank,

153

empty space where his friend should be, and the emptiness stabbed Henry like a sword.

It's my fault.

Before their eyes, the dinosaur melted back into a dragon—a dragon without wings, without teeth, without claws, without a tail. It puffed a furious puff through its nostrils and then held its breath, and its dragon face flamed red with effort as it pushed all of its energy into changing shape once more—what little shape was left. Its body was a hulking mass of scales. One muscular leg ended in a sharp-toed foot. Out of the dragon's forehead grew a horn—longer, longer, longer—a flashing, razor-tipped horn stolen from a unicorn Henry had once drawn on his door. It glittered like glass and cut the air like a knife. The unicorn horn and the stomping, jumping dragon foot and the eyes flaming with anger—Henry thought he had never seen such a lumpy, misshapen, deadly picture in his life.

"It's—it's like a Jabberwock!" said Jade.

"A what?" said Henry.

"Don't you know the poem 'Jabberwocky'? It's all about a courageous boy who goes to fight a dangerous creature in the woods . . .

The Jabberwock, with eyes of flame,
Came whiffling through the tulgey wood,
And burbled as it came!

The sounds coming from the dragon did sound a lot like whiffling and burbling. But Henry felt himself growing taller and stronger inside, and his armor shone more brightly than ever, and he was not afraid. Not even the good kind of afraid. He *was* a courageous boy, wasn't he? Maybe the poem was about him.

"The boy defeats the Jabberwock with a vorpal blade," said Jade. "Do you have a vorpal blade? That's what the poem says:

One, two! One, two! And through and through
The vorpal blade went snicker-snack!
He left it dead, and with its head
He went galumphing back.

Henry did not know what a vorpal blade was, nor where to find one in an elementary school cafeteria. But Jade was already searching through all of the drawers and cabinets in the kitchen. "Here!" she called, and she held up a cheese grater. It was covered with little pokey pieces of metal—like a sword with teeth. Then she pulled out of the refrigerator a wheel of cheese and stuck a fork in the back of it to use as a handle. "Your shield, Sir Henry!"

Could he do this? Was he brave enough? Was he strong enough? Could he go galumphing back? He peeked inside his armor.

TIE YOUR SHOELACES.

Yes. He was, and he could. He bent down and tied his shoelaces. Then he switched his cowboy hat for his knight's helmet. He took the cheese-grater sword and the cheese-wheel shield and turned to face his stomping, snorting enemy.

The dragon attacked, swinging its horn and hopping from side to side on its one leg like a bull on a pogo stick. Henry braced himself behind his shield. His feet were as quick as Q-tips in a tornado. His sword was as swift and swishy as a hummingbird caught in a washing machine.

CLANG! CRACK! CRUNCH! SLRRRRMPSH!

Orange bits flew in all directions as the unicorn's horn sliced through the wheel of cheese.

One-two, one-two! went his vorpal blade. Little shavings of grated horn fell to the floor.

The horn came whipping sideways at him. He ducked and rolled over, then leaped to his feet. "Aha! You're going to be tricky, are you? Well, let's see if you can dodge my super sneaky sideways sword swipe!"

Snicker-snack!

Jade clapped and burst into song.

> *"Sir Henry Penwhistle!" the people cheered.*
> *"The bravest knight that ever lacked a beard!*
> *He'll save us with a snicker and a snack.*
> *He'll whack that dragon with a thund'rous whack.*
> *There's no doubt he will come galumphing back!"*

"What is going on?" wailed the Lunch Lady. "Someone tell me what is happening! Oh, I'm going to end up back at Waffle Heaven, I just know it."

From one corner of the cafeteria to the other, the two opponents hopped and clomped and clattered. Their feet pounded the battlefield. Henry felt a glow of light around him, giving him courage. And then, with a whizzy sort of whisper, the horn went *wsssshhh* and then *whhhheee* and sliced a little circle in the front of Henry's armor.

The middle of the circle fell out, and Henry could see a hole right over his heart.

"Hey!"

The unicorn-dragon looked almost as surprised as Henry. They both stared at the hole and then at the silvery shape on the floor. And the battlefield was only a cold carpet of sandwich crusts and dried-up blobs of jelly. And the light was only the hot glare of lightbulbs shining off plastic spinach leaves. And his armor, his *invincible* armor, was only a raincoat covered in aluminum foil, with an O-shaped emptiness.

O for Oscar.

Henry lost his balance and sat down. Hard.

This wasn't like play-fighting in his bedroom. This was real. Suddenly it was much, much too real. *I want to start the day over again*, he thought. But the day was too thick around him to erase now. It was like a cloud of chalk dust making his eyes water and his nose run. And now his Work of Art was about to slice up his chivalry piece by piece.

This was real, but *he* wasn't real. He was only a pretend knight, with a pretend sword.

He could hear Jade singing behind him,

O stars, O paper moons, O pizza guys,
O plastic eggplant swinging from the skies,
Come quickly now, don't tarry, heed our woe!
Bring strength! bring wisdom! 'til our fearsome foe
Is hurled to deepest deeps, the battle won,
And brave Sir Henry shineth like the sun!

She was standing on the counter, her hands clenched at her sides. Her face glistened as she sent poetry flying at the dragon. She was fighting the battle with her words. But Henry no longer believed those golden words were about him. He felt the *Sir* tumbling away. He was only Henry. And he wanted Oscar back.

Henry's toe nudged the little piece of armor that had fallen to the floor, and it turned over. There were words in red ink:

DON'T RUN AWAY.

He thought of St. George and that other dragon. He thought of Luke Skywalker and Darth Vader. He thought of Peter Pan and Captain Hook. He thought of David and Goliath.

"Perambulating lobe-sniffer!"

Henry nearly dropped the cheese grater, for those were

not the words of Jade *or* the Lunch Lady. That was the muffled voice of Oscar, Oscar with all of the best insults, insulting the dragon from inside the dragon's belly. Or was he insulting Henry? It didn't matter.

"Oscar!" Henry cried.

"Warthog! Wombat!" came the muffled voice again. "Knucklehead! Gnatcatcher!"

"Nincompoop!" Henry yelled at the top of his lungs.

Henry stood up.

He set his helmet straight.

He raised his shield.

Jade fell silent, and even the Lunch Lady in her prison held her breath and listened. All Henry could hear was the pattering of his heart (or was it the dragon's heart?) like the ticking of Captain Hook's crocodile: *tick-tock, tick-tock, tick-tock*.

The dragon lowered its horn and took aim, but Henry did not run away. It galloped a hopping gallop, but Henry did not run away. It snorted and smoked and growled a terrible growl, but Henry—*Sir* Henry—did not run away. And then it rammed its glittery point straight through Henry's shield—

—and got stuck.

Halted. Jammed. Bamboozled. Gummed up inside a gigantic cheese.

The dragon reared its head, tossing Henry into the air. But Henry held on tightly to the cheese-covered horn and dug his shoes into the dragon's eyes. The dragon whipped its head around blindly. Its belly heaved. Henry could feel the flames burning and building inside the dragon, rolling toward its throat.

"Help me!" Henry yelled.

Jade leaped onto the dragon's leg. Thrown off balance, the dragon fell.

Its weight made the floor tremble in fear. The ceiling lights jiggled in triumph.

And then the dragon roared a sad, pleading roar that echoed in Henry's chest. A hole appeared in its stomach. The hole got bigger, and bigger. Out of the hole came a hand holding an eraser, and then Oscar tumbled out, looking dazed and dizzy and ash-covered from fiery dragon breath but wholly, wonderfully himself. His gaze turned from Henry to the hole in the dragon's belly and back to Henry again. He breathed slowly. "That was *awesome*!"

Chapter 14
Henry's Idea

"*O FRABJOUS DAY! Callooh! Callay!*" sang Jade, dancing with the half-chewed plastic vegetables and twirling the fallen banner in circles around her head.

Henry flew at Oscar like a bowling ball hurled into a rainbow sunset, and they melted to the floor together, laughing and wrestling. He squeezed and squeezed, as if to make sure that his friend was real—that the hole in the world had been filled again. Beside them, the dragon was struggling to change one more time. It was curling and stretching and bulging with possible shapes—an airplane, a tarantula, a fire engine, a robot—but there were too many pieces missing.

"Oscar!" cried the Lunch Lady. "Oh please, please tell me . . . are the pizzas safe?"

From the direction of the kitchen they could hear the faint sound of chewing. "Uh oh," said Oscar, and he ran to investigate. Jade and Henry followed. The counter was empty except for a little sprinkle of crumbs. The octagon was lying on the floor, as big as a garbage can lid, munching on the last pepperoni. Twenty-five big circles and 396 little circles—all gone.

Oscar groaned. "I'll see if there's more in the refrigerator."

"We'll rescue the Lunch Lady!" said Jade, and she and Henry ran over to the tower of tables. But the tables were too huge and too heavy. They pushed, they pulled, they took running leaps and slammed their bodies against the tabletops. Jade yelled, "FORSOOTH!" as loud as she could, hoping the sound waves would topple the pile. But nothing worked. What they needed, Henry thought, was a strongman—one of those big, muscular circus men who lift cannons and cars full of clowns.

And all at once they heard a shrill voice soaring behind them, rising almost to the tipping point of tears: "You *wanted* the dinosaur to eat me!"

Henry felt something sharp deep inside his chest, as if he had swallowed the cheese grater instead of fighting bravely with it. He turned around.

Oscar was standing in the doorway to the kitchen, holding the sketchbook, which Henry had left on the floor with his backpack while he fought the dinosaur-dragon-Jabberwock. The sketchbook was open in Oscar's hands, and Henry didn't have to guess what page was showing.

"You *wanted* it to eat me," Oscar repeated. "You drew it that way."

"No, I didn't!" said Henry quickly. "I was mad the day I drew that. I'm sorry. I wish I hadn't drawn it."

"But you did."

Henry ran to where Oscar was standing. He tore the page out of the sketchbook and ripped it into little pieces. But he knew that wouldn't make it better. He could erase something, he could tear it up, but he couldn't *undraw* it. He couldn't *unimagine* it.

"I'm sorry," Henry said.

"And anyway," sputtered Oscar, "a *Stegosaurus* is an *herbivore*! It eats plants, not people! You *never* get dinosaurs right." Setting his jaw firmly, he picked up the eraser and stomped over to where the dragon lay.

"Wait!" called Henry.

The dragon had stopped trying to change shapes. It was lying still. Its belly heaved with exhaustion. Little steaming tears dribbled out of its eyes, fell to the floor, and sizzled. No teeth. No claws. No legs. No wings. No fiery breath. Just a big jungle-green blob with a sorry face. Squiggles and lines and color. Defeated at last.

Henry had never felt like such a villain in all his life. "Wait! Don't erase it!"

Oscar turned and stared at him, and Henry saw steaming dragon tears in his eyes too. "You let it eat me," said Oscar. "And now you don't want to erase it? You care more about the dragon than about your *best friend*?"

Henry couldn't explain it—how awful it felt to see something he had made, something he had shaped with his own hands, lying there like a squeezed-out lemon. He had loved that picture on his door. It had come out of his imagination. It was his own fault that the dragon was so fierce and fearsome and full of fire.

But he had done what a knight was supposed to do. He had saved the day. And then he had ruined the day. Why did he feel as if the cheese grater was grating his insides into little pieces?

"I'm going to erase it," said Oscar, turning back towards the dragon.

Henry pulled the eraser out of Oscar's hand and threw it as hard as he could. The eraser sailed over their heads and landed on the hat of the popsicle-stick farmer, who didn't show any intention of giving it back.

The two boys stared at each other darkly.

"It was a stupid, ugly picture," said Oscar. Henry knew Oscar must be very, very mad to use words like "stupid" and "ugly" instead of fancier insults like *muttonheaded* or *grotesque*. And for some reason, those simple words hurt Henry more than any of the fancier ones would have.

"At least I can draw something better than an *octagon*!" Henry sputtered before he could stop himself. "That's not even a thing. It's just a shape." And instantly he wished he could unsay it, just like he wished he could undraw the worst-friend picture. Oscar's face was screwed up into a twisty shape and he blinked his eyes hard, which Henry knew meant he was refusing to cry.

"It is *too* a thing," said Oscar. "It's *my* thing. And anyway,

I didn't draw it. I grew it in a petri dish. So it's *real*."

"What's a petri dish?" asked Jade, who had been standing quietly, watching their argument with a frown.

"It's a round glass dish with bacteria-food in it where organisms grow in a laboratory," said Oscar.

"Maybe that's why the octagon likes to eat circles," said Jade. "They remind it of home cooking."

Oscar ignored her and stomped toward the kitchen. "I'm going to go do an experiment. Don't disturb me."

But something was stuck inside Henry's throat, and it had to come out. "You *laughed* at me! Friends aren't supposed to laugh at friends!"

Oscar looked back at him with a look frosty enough to freeze a supernova. "Ha. HA." Then he disappeared into the kitchen.

Henry started to follow him, but Jade quietly shook her head. He wanted to ask her, *Are there any more epic poems for me? Can I ever be a hero, ever? Is my quest over?* He wanted her to start singing those golden words again, but when he opened his mouth, his words wouldn't behave. "Are you sure you're not a government spy or an alien plotting to steal earthlings?"

Jade tapped one finger on her forehead as if to think about this. "Yes. I am sure."

"Then why are you always watching us?"

"Because," she sighed, "*sometimes* you are *interesting.*"

Suddenly the booming voice of Mr. Bruce echoed through the cafeteria: "I heard the cries of a damsel in distress, and I came as fast as I could . . . luckily I was already inside the school, but I shaved off ten pounds getting through that hole in the top of the door!" Henry whirled around. Even soaking wet, the bus driver was a magnificent sight. His eyes were all smiles and kindness, and his feet were big and dusty and quick, and his arms could have lifted three lions, an elephant, and a circus tent to boot. He was a muscle sandwich. He was just the person Henry needed to tear down the table fortress.

"Mr. Bruce—the Lunch Lady! She's trapped underneath all the tables. Can you move them?"

"Well, that's what I'm here for!" cried the bus driver. He took one long look at the shivering dragon blob in the middle of the room and raised his eyebrows at Henry, but Mr. Bruce was a man who did his work before asking questions. He ran to the tower of tables. "Don't you worry, fair

damsel," he said, pulling down tables. "I'm going to get you out of there."

The last of the tables tumbled away, and the Lunch Lady rose slowly, stumbling a little, trying to straighten the scrambled yellow mess of her hair. "Mr. Bruce, you are my hero. I must look like a Jackson Pollock painting—all tumbled and tangled and squiggly."

"Miss Brie, my darling," said Mr. Bruce, "if I made a statue of cinnamon sticks, with eyes of blueberries and cheeks of apple cobbler and golden gumdrops in its hair, and if I loved that statue so much that it turned into a real live person, it would look just like you."

"Oh, for goodness' sake," said the Lunch Lady, bashfully hiding her nose behind her frying pan.

"Miss Brie?" whispered Henry. He never knew the Lunch Lady had a name. *"My darling?"* He wrinkled his nose.

"And that," whispered Jade, "is why I will never be a damsel in distress. Why do they always say *damsel* in distress anyway? As if *girls* are the ones who are always getting themselves into trouble! Ridiculous. Why don't you ever hear about all the *boys* in distress?" She sighed. "I've got a lot of rescuing to do."

Henry didn't say anything, but he remembered her leaping with an eraser onto the tail of a flying *Stegosaurus*, and he smiled. She was good, this new girl. She could command an army. She could probably even write a book.

Just then the Lunch Lady saw the state of her surroundings. Tables and chairs were tipped over and scattered everywhere. Plastic vegetables were trampled into colorful pulp on the floor. The NATIONAL VEGETABLE WEEK banner was lying in a heap. The eggplant drawings on the walls and half the hanging art projects were gone—eaten.

"My *art show*!" Miss Brie wailed.

"Don't you worry about it, Miss Brie," said Mr. Bruce. "There's plenty more creativity where all *that* came from."

But Miss Brie was already running in the other direction. "My *kitchen*!" she wailed.

"I'm conducting an *experiment*," Oscar protested.

"It's a wreck!"

"It's SCIENCE!"

Mr. Bruce chuckled. Then he turned and looked again at the creature in the middle of the cafeteria. His forehead folded into a frown.

TELL THE TRUTH. Henry was so tired of those orange words. His chivalry was wearing thin.

"It's a dragon," he said, watching Mr. Bruce's face closely. "Well, it *was* a dragon, before most of it got erased. I drew it on my bedroom door, but I guess I drew it too well because it didn't want to get erased, so it escaped and took all of my other drawings with it, and we had to chase it all over the school." His words seemed to be chasing each other out of his mouth. "And then it ate Oscar, which was my fault because I drew that too, but it's okay because Oscar erased his way out again only now he's mad at me and I don't want to erase the dragon but I've got to erase the dragon because I'm a knight and that's what knights do."

Mr. Bruce slapped his knee and laughed his mountainous laugh. "Well, if that isn't the darnedest thing!" Henry didn't think it was *that* funny. But Mr. Bruce's laughter was different from other people's. He wasn't laughing *at* Henry. He was inviting Henry to laugh too.

He believes me, thought Henry. And suddenly the bus driver's presence felt like a door opening—a bus door, crinkling to let him inside so he could scrunch down into a seat and bury his head in his armor and ride to a new place, a new adventure. He could feel his nose filling up and his eyes burning and his lips swelling, which made him angry, because there was no way he would cry in front of Jade— not in a million gazillion years. "I'm never going to draw anything ever again," he said, and squeezed the crying back inside his face. "Never ever. I won't ever imagine anything, if this is what comes out. I'll just think about NOTHING all the time!"

"Well, now, don't be so quick to say that," said Mr. Bruce, scratching his chin. "A story escaped from me once, and you wouldn't believe the trouble it caused! It jumped in a woman's purse and stowed away to the post office. Then it hitchhiked on a stamped envelope to the mayor's office. Then it piggybacked on the mayor's cat to the grocery store. Then it hopped from hat to hat to hat all the way from one end of town to the other. I spent weeks running around cleaning up the messes it had made. Just goes to show that you never know. You never know. But it sure doesn't stop me from telling stories."

"I wish I knew the rules," said Henry. Was there a chivalry for drawing things? He knew it wasn't good chivalry to draw a dinosaur eating your best friend, but did chivalry mean always drawing cute bunnies? Did chivalry mean always keeping your door locked so that your dragon could never escape? Did it mean keeping your quest hidden safely under the bed?

"Once you make something," continued Mr. Bruce, "a picture, or a story, or a song, or an invention, or even a delicious meal, it isn't yours anymore. It has a life. It could spend its life lying quietly on your paper, staring up at you and saying, 'Thank you for drawing me. Aren't I wonderful?' Or it could fill the stomach of a queen or give strength to a poor man in the street. It could wrap itself around a city and make the people in it cry an ocean, or it could wiggle into the ears of a baby and make her burst into giggles."

"I know what you mean," said Jade. "Sometimes when I sing, the song takes off on its own. Listen." Jade took a deep breath.

"*Hum-de-dum-de-do-dah!*" she sang. Nothing happened.

"*E-i-e-i-o!*" she sang again. Still nothing happened.

"*FalalalaLAAAAAAAA!*" she sang again. And this time, the song burst out of her mouth like a cannonball and soared across the cafeteria, bouncing off the walls and the ceiling lights. It shot out the hole in the cafeteria door, and they could hear a chorus of splashes and more and more voices singing, *"FalalalaLAAAAAAAA!"*

"See?" Jade said excitedly.

"That's right," said Mr. Bruce. "All you can do is make the best thing you can, and love it as hard as you can, and let it go loose in the world, and watch what happens." His voice grew quiet and urgent. "Henry, let your imagination be as wild as the spinning universe. Let it be beautiful and adventurous and even terrifying. Let it go free. Don't be afraid. But remember that art does things you don't expect. Remember that it can hurt people, but remember that it can make them happy as well. Remember that it can break things and stomp on things sometimes, and that's where chivalry comes in— the good knight in your heart. What kind of art is that good knight brave enough to make?"

"I don't know," mumbled Henry. He fumbled at the sleeve of his raincoat.

"You have to be brave to be an artist. You have to squeeze your fear down deep in your chest, and make something new."

Make something new. Suddenly Henry forgot to think about Nothing. Suddenly his mind was full of whirling, swirling shapes.

"I have an idea!" he yelled.

"Good heavens!" said Mr. Bruce. "Stupendous! Calloo! Callay! Sally forth, Sir Henry, and *create*!"

"But first I have to go to the supply closet." Henry ran to the cafeteria door and then halted in his tracks. "Uh oh."

Jade, running after, nearly bumped into him. "Whoa."

Henry had forgotten that there was a whole world of problems beyond his epic battle with the dragon. And that world was swirling right past the broken window at the top of the cafeteria door, through which they had come. The dishrags the Lunch Lady had stuffed into the cracks around and under the door were soaked through, and a pool of water was spreading across the floor. Henry and Jade waded through the puddle, stood on their tiptoes, and peeked out the window.

The hallway was a rushing river, and just about everyone and everything in the school was being swept along in the current. The water was filled with paper and pens and books and backpacks. Whole classes were sailing along on desks and chairs, reciting multiplication tables. Students having a science lesson about frogs were trying to catch the ones that escaped into the water. The kindergartners were paddling on their cafeteria trays and singing "Itsy Bitsy Spider" at the top of their lungs. Mr. Boolean, the librarian, glided through the water on a huge world atlas, open to the South America page, while he held up a map of the Galapagos Islands as a sail. Principal Bunk floated by, still stuck to his chair, talking on the phone with the Bored Members and assuring them that yes, yes, everything was fine, it was just a normal, educational day at the Safest Elementary School in the County.

"Good luck out there!" laughed Mr. Bruce. "I had to sail around the whole school thirteen times and nearly got drowned under a floating pile of spelling tests before I finally caught hold of the right door!"

"Cockamamie bumber . . . bubble," Henry groaned, wishing Oscar were beside him to properly insult the catastrophe. He leaned his head against the door.

"I have an idea," said Jade, "but we'll need Oscar's octagon."

CHAPTER 15
JADE'S IDEA

"NO WAY," said Oscar.

Henry and Jade crouched down beside him. He was sitting on the floor stroking his octagon protectively. Around them the kitchen looked like a piece of Swiss cheese, with perfect round holes in the counters and the cabinet doors. Miss Brie was busily covering the holes up with aluminum foil, so that the entire kitchen seemed to be wearing a suit of armor. Apparently Oscar's scientific experiment was not going well. Or perhaps it was going *too* well. He stuck a finger in the pizza sauce and drew a circle on a cookie sheet. The octagon ate a hole right through it.

"But Oscar, it's the only thing that can help us," pleaded Henry.

"I thought it was *just a shape*. Not like a *dragon* or something *important* like that."

"I didn't mean that. Oscar, I'm sorry. I really, really am."

Oscar looked so green with grumpiness that he would have turned into the Incredible Hulk right then and there if his mother had not made him wear a shirt with so many buttons that morning. "How come you're taking *her* idea?" He didn't look at Jade.

"Because—" Henry suddenly felt shy.

Jade jumped in, "Oscar, just think of it: later on, when people are telling stories of the incredible battle with the dragon at La Muncha Elementary School, this will be the stuff of legend. Your octagon will be immortalized in epic verse for centuries to come."

"Yeah, because of that," said Henry, gratefully.

Oscar paused and then nodded, and some of the greenness faded from his face. "Okay, but you better not hurt it."

Ten minutes later, he almost did burst through his buttons. "You killed it!" he wailed.

"I did not kill it," said Jade calmly.

"Yes, you did. There's blood all over it!"

"That's not blood. It's ketchup."

Jade had stuck the octagon onto Miss Brie's frying pan with chewing gum, covered it with ketchup, and written the word STOP on it with her finger.

Mr. Bruce peeked over her shoulder. "Now that," he said, "is the most heroic octagon I have ever seen."

Oscar sniffed and checked to make sure there were no serious wounds, then followed the others out of the kitchen.

"But what will I serve for lunch?" asked Miss Brie, blinking back tears and blowing her nose in a napkin. "Everyone will be expecting a pizza party, and there's no pizza."

"There's lots more food in the refrigerator," said Jade. "Well, lots of *not* pizza. "

"I," said Mr. Bruce, smiling, "know for a fact that you are an *artist* with food. Why, I've seen you take a roast chicken and shape it into a sculpture worthy of the finest museums of Europe!"

"But not here," Miss Brie sniffed. "Not at La Muncha Elementary School. Here everyone wants pizza, and meat-loaf, and macaroni and cheese made from a box. A *box*! How can anything beautiful come from a box?"

Henry agreed.

"I think you're keeping all your talent hidden," said Mr. Bruce, smiling, "like Henry and his sketchbook."

"Remember," said Jade, "you have to be brave to be an artist."

Miss Brie stood up straight and smoothed down her apron. Her peach-colored cheeks flushed with new excitement. "You're right. I'll do it. I'll show this school what Vegetable Art *really* looks like! My pencil will be a chef's knife. My paintbrush will be a spatula. My canvas will be a pile of empty plates. La Muncha, get ready to *eat*."

And so, while Mr. Bruce sat on the dragon's belly and told it stories, and Miss Brie went into a clatter of cooking, Henry, Oscar, and Jade looked out the window at the top of the cafeteria door.

"Your shoe touched my foot," said Oscar.

"Then stand somewhere else," said Henry.

Oscar muttered under his breath, "Jurassic gingko."

Henry retorted, "*Humuhumunukunukuapuaa*," and he thought he saw a little wiggle of a smile tickle the corner of Oscar's mouth. And suddenly that made him enormously happy. "Let's go!"

Jade held the octagon disguised as a STOP sign out the window.

With a mighty SLUUUUUUURP, everything and everyone in the hallway *stopped*. The water curled upward into a wet, whirling wall. The people on their makeshift boats all halted in a line right in front of the STOP sign. The books and desks and frogs and people behind *them* bumped into the line, and so on and so forth, until there was a muddle of stopped teachers and students getting more and more tangled up and angry. Now there was a clear, dry path for Henry across the hallway. It was like Moses parting the Red Sea—if the Red Sea had been full of pencils and kindergartners.

"That was *not* scientific," said Oscar.

"That was *awesome*," said Henry.

"My mom says nobody can ignore a stop sign," said Jade.

As awesome as it was, the sight of the growing wall of water made Henry hesitate. Could it hold still? How long *would* water obey a heroic-octagon-stop-sign? He shook off his nervousness—he'd just defeated a dragon, for goodness' sake!—and jumped out of the window.

In seconds he was across the hallway, filling his backpack

with things he needed from the supply closet—glue, feathers, markers, paint, play dough, a package of one hundred paper cups, and much more. He took down one of the plastic containers full of paper and slid it towards the cafeteria door. Oscar scrambled out the window and handed the container to Jade. But before Henry could follow Oscar back through the window into the cafeteria, he heard gasps coming from above his head. The wall of water and stopped people and scrambled stuff was like a dam about to burst. On the very top of the pile, Miss Pimpernel's class sat on their bulletin-board-raft.

"Henry, did you catch the dragon?"

"Henry, are you really a knight?"

"I'm—" Henry gulped. "I'm going to finish our Art Project."

"Wait for us!"

And suddenly Henry was nearly squashed to death under all of the arms and legs and noses of his classmates as they jumped on top of him.

The octagon growled.

"Halt, children! Don't you see the STOP sign?" called Miss Pimpernel. The children ignored her. Even the big red letters inside Henry's armor—**ALWAYS STOP AT A STOP SIGN**—ignored her. "Someday when you are teenagers and fail your driving tests, don't come back complaining that I didn't teach you anything!"

Henry saw Simon Snoot still peeking over the edge of the raft. His face was a storm. He stared down at Henry, then at Miss Pimpernel.

And he jumped.

One by one the students climbed into the cafeteria. Then Jade pulled the octagon back in, and the dam burst, and everyone and everything else went rushing down the hallway again.

"Wait!" called Miss Pimpernel, looking over her shoulder at her students as the raft rushed forward. "Wait for me!"

CHAPTER 16
THE MASTERPIECE

HENRY'S CLASSMATES swarmed around the lumpy shape in the middle of the cafeteria. Mr. Bruce was sitting beside it reciting the poem "Jabberwocky." Miss Brie was heaping spoonfuls of scrambled eggs into its mouth. It licked its green lips.

"What is it?" the children asked.

"It's an armless, legless, tailless, toothless, wingless, fire-less dragon," whispered Henry.

"Awesome!" A little whirlwind of hands began poking it and pinching it.

"You can't touch a dragon unless you're a knight," Henry said quickly.

"Make me a knight! Oh, please, make me a knight!" They were crowding around him now, their faces squeezing all the air out of him. Where did Oscar go? He needed Oscar to do the talking. He looked to Mr. Bruce for help, but Mr. Bruce was just smiling, waiting, listening.

He pulled his head and his hands into his armor like a turtle and made the rest of the world disappear. He had tracked a disguised dragon all over the school. He had scolded a U.S. president and had sailed a ship. He had faced a pair of giant cowboy boots and a flying dinosaur and a unicorn horn. What were his own classmates compared to all of that?

BE BRAVE said the green pencil. I *am* brave, said Henry.

BE KIND said the purple crayon.

He peeked out of the hole the dragon had sliced in his armor.

There was Trina with her bag of marshmallows and her enormous toothy grin that seemed bigger than all of the rest of her, like the Cheshire Cat in *Alice in Wonderland*.

There was Louie, with a brain he didn't know he had yet, like the Scarecrow in *The Wizard of Oz*. There was Katie with her trumpet and Drew with his kazoo. There were Norman, Nelson, and Neville, each trying to be the one in front. There was Jade smiling her sideways smile and tossing her purple scarf over her shoulder—not an alien, not a spy, not a new girl, but a poet and a friend. There they all were—tall, short, round, noodly, pokey, dimply, golden, greenish, brownish, bluish—so many shapes, like perfect drawings that had popped off someone's painted door. They were Works of Art.

And so Henry pulled his head out of his armor, and he dubbed them knights, every one—even the girls, even Jade (especially Jade). And then he dumped the container full of art supplies into the middle of the floor. "Okay, are you ready to draw?"

But Simon Snoot stepped forward, crossed his arms, and smirked at Henry. "Even if this *is* all real (though I still think someone's playing a trick on us), I thought we were going to *fight*. I thought we were *knights*. Art is for wimps."

"No it's not!" It was Oscar this time, stomping forward and holding something tightly in his arms. "Sir Henry defeated the dragon AND he's the best artist in the world. Look at *this*." And before Henry could lunge forward and grab it away, Oscar was in the midst of everyone, showing off his sketchbook. Henry turned bright red, and then purple. He tried very hard to turn green. Oscar had *no right* to show his secret book. That was *his* adventure, and nobody else's.

A wave of knights swirled around the pages of *Sir Henry's Quest*.

"WOW!"

"Look at that spider!"

"Look at the rhinoceros! It looks so real it could jump off the page!"

"It gives me goosebumps."

"Is that Abraham Lincoln?"

"I wish I could draw like that. I would draw and draw and never stop."

"Wow, Henry, these are really *good*!"

And no one, not a single person, was laughing. Even Simon Snoot looked impressed.

Henry felt Mr. Bruce's firm hand on his shoulder. "You see, Henry? I told you not to keep all of that imagination hidden. It's time to open the door and let it out!"

All of his creations, all of his shapes and imaginings, roaming free for everyone to see? It was terrifying. And yet there was his army of knights, looking at him as if he were a superhero with a magic pencil—as if he could save the world just by drawing it.

"I have an idea!" said Oscar. "We can make a rocket ship out of thousands of paper airplanes all glued together and put the dragon-blob-thing inside, and we can use the octagon as a trampoline and make the rocket ship bounce and bounce on it until it shoots right through the roof all the way to the moon."

"No, no, no! I have a better idea," said Henry. "We're going to make the dragon all over again."

"*What?*"

"Only it's going to be different this time. It's going to be New. Here's what I want you all to do . . ." And he took the sketchbook and set it on the floor, and all of the children gathered around him, and he turned the pages one by one and explained.

"OH, MY," said a voice behind them all.

They turned, and there stood Miss Pimpernel. Her hair

had come unwound from its neat bun and stood out from her head stiffly like a flaming copper crown. Water poured from her skirt. Her chest was heaving (*Could she possibly have swum upstream?* thought Henry), and the three freckles quivered and danced on her chin. "Oh . . . ," she whispered, shaking so much that Henry ran over to grab her before she toppled over like a tree. "Oh my."

"Miss Pimpernel!" He held her arm tightly, but she didn't seem to see him. She was gazing around the cafeteria—at the children bending over the sketchbook, at the bus driver and the Lunch Lady, at the disheveled vegetable art splattered across the floor, and at the giant mound of half-erased jungle-green dragon in the middle of it all.

"Miss Pimpernel," Henry said again, and she finally looked down at him. "What superhero did you used to be, before you were a teacher?"

"I . . . I was—" A wave of a memory swept across her face, and when it passed, there was a smile on her lips that Henry had never seen before. Gently pushing away his hands, she walked over to the box of art supplies and reached in. "I," she said, pulling out a bottle of glue and holding it up high, "was the Super-Gluer."

For the next hour, the cafeteria was a tornado of painting and cutting and molding and twisting and licking and stamping and folding and coloring and gluing. Henry ran back and forth, helping out here, drawing something there, giving directions, answering questions, handing out praise, and talking so much that he wondered whether his tongue had turned into a race car. The words flew out of his mouth the way Jade's song had flown out of hers. They were like little winds making a dozen windmills spin—they made people scurry, and they made people scribble, and they made people smile.

"Do you want the feet to be like a mallard or an American wigeon?"

"What?" Henry stared at Simon Snoot, who was staring back at him quite seriously.

"A mallard's feet are orange, and an American wigeon's feet are bluish-grey."

"You know a lot about ducks," said Henry.

Simon crossed his arms. "I *aced* the test on animals. I know a lot about armadillos too. And platypuses. And eels. And beavers. And lions."

And crickets, Henry thought.

"I know a lot about a lot of things."

BE KIND.

Henry imagined all the animals gathering around Simon, whispering secrets in his ear, making him the new king of Narnia. "Well, I guess you can decide, then."

"Great!" Simon grinned and ran back to his spot. And for the first time ever, his nose didn't look in the slightest bit smooshed. His eyes weren't rolling. His mouth wasn't smirking. Was his face changing shape? It looked almost—*nice*.

Marybeth, princess Marybeth, soon to be queen of the Butterfly People, waved Henry over to her corner. "Can I make the wings pink?" she asked.

He gazed at her in horror. He thought about all the sacrifices that great heroes had to make and all the things they had to suffer—hunger and cold and nightmares and monsters and lost friends and lost treasure and loneliness and sickness and the whole world making fun of them. A knight must do what a knight must do, but some things just go too far.

BE KIND. BE KIND. BE KIND.

"How about yellow?" Henry asked.

Marybeth thought for a minute. "Okay!" she said.

Jade drew hundreds and hundreds of stars on construction paper and hid them inside the scrambled eggs that Miss Brie was feeding to the dragon. It ate and ate and ate until it couldn't squeeze in one more bite. Then it burped and smiled in contentment.

Around them all Miss Pimpernel flitted with her bottle of glue, binding the torn things, fixing the broken things, joining the separate things, and doing what she had always done—making things stick. Shining from her face was the New Smile. Henry would have to come up with a name for that smile, someday, when she had worn it long enough.

And all the while Mr. Bruce was telling them a story by someone named Edward Lear about some people called the Jumblies who had green heads and blue hands and sailed away to the Torrible Zone and the Chankly Bore, which made everyone laugh. And at last, they were finished.

And they put down the markers and paintbrushes and scissors and glue.

And they stood back to look at their Art Project.

This wasn't just a dragon. This was a Masterpiece.

It had the webbed feet of a duck, one orange, one bluish-grey. Its arms were the long, wavy, wiggly arms of an octopus, covered with zillions of paper cups like little suckers. Where its horns used to be, a shiny golden trumpet and a big red kazoo stuck out of the top of its head. When it opened its mouth to roar, two gleaming white rows of marshmallow teeth peeked out. It had a peacock's tail—a fan of green and purple feathers, covered with circles that looked like eyes peering out in all directions. Sprouting from its back were two enormous yellow butterfly wings, and they were almost the best thing of all, because on them the class had drawn . . . bunnies.

But not ordinary bunnies. No, these bunnies had robot laser eyes. There were bunnies with tall Abraham Lincoln hats and penguin suits. There were pirate bunnies and cowboy bunnies and Tarzan bunnies and superhero bunnies. There were bunnies kicking soccer balls and bunnies digging up dinosaur bones and bunnies eating pizzas and bunnies flying spaceships to Mars. There were purple bunnies with carrot ears and orange bunnies with potato feet and polka-dot bunnies with cauliflower tails and striped bunnies with cucumber noses. Each one was different.

And when the dragon waved its wings, they were a hundred colors and too many shapes to count.

"Oh," sighed Miss Pimpernel, clasping her hands on her chest as if her heart would explode with joy. "Oh, I do adore bunnies."

And Sir Henry Penwhistle looked at the dragon and loved it. It was the most marvelous thing he had ever seen. It was what he had always *meant* to draw, but he never knew it until now.

Like most masterpieces, the dragon was at first not sure of its own quality. It licked its marshmallow teeth thoughtfully and a strange smile spread over its face.

It did a little dance on its duck feet. The class screamed with laughter.

It swiveled its peacock tail around so all you could see of it were eyes, and eyes, and more eyes—enough eyes to see all the way to another solar system. The class hooted and clapped and cheered.

Its trumpet horn played "The Star-Spangled Banner," and its kazoo horn (which sounded like a singing zipper) played "On Top of Spaghetti." The class sang along.

It reached out its octopus arms and sucked up half a

dozen students with its suction cups and whirled them around and around and around in the air.

This was better than any X-treme Turbo-robotic Nano-knuckle Anti-gravity Thunder-crusher on the planet.

Then the strangest thing started happening. The more the dragon waved its new wings and stomped its new feet and whirled its new arms, the more real they looked. The new parts seemed to grow into the dragon, not like paper and clay and feathers glued on, but like its very own self.

"Is it magic?" whispered Jade.

"Magic?" said Mr. Bruce. "Of course it's not magic. It's art!"

The class was having so much fun with the new dragon they hardly noticed that a crowd was gathering. More students had begun escaping from the flooded hallway, and they were sloshing, wet and bedraggled, into the cafeteria. And what a sight greeted them!

"What is it? What is it?" they yelled. They began clambering onto the dragon's back and begging for a turn swinging on the octopus arms.

Miss Brie hurried back into the kitchen. And no one at La Muncha Elementary School—indeed no one in the entire town of Squashbuckle—could have imagined the things she brought out next: Carrots carved into orange alligators swimming in ponds of peanut butter. Zucchini pirate ships with sails made of spinach leaves held up by toothpicks, and little sausage pirates rowing celery-stick oars. Chicken soup with green bean Loch Ness monsters poking their heads out. Knobbly-headed squash people with radish-slice eyes and tomato-slice smiles. Plates and plates of beautiful deliciousness. And the children ate and ate and ate.

"Welcome to my art show!" the Lunch Lady said at last, spreading her arms wide and looking as happy as a baked sunrise pudding. "I am pleased to announce that First Place goes to Miss Pimpernel's class for the New Dragon, who has recently become a vegetarian. I'm especially impressed with the vegetable-bunnies on the dragon's wings. Notice the cauliflower tails. They look good enough to eat!" She pinned a blue ribbon to the dragon's chest, and the dragon was greatly admired and applauded by one and all.

Just then they heard a voice echoing from the hallway, *"Falalalala . . ."* Jade's song was bouncing back. It grew louder and deeper, like a thunderous wave of joy billowing towards them. It burst into the cafeteria and flew over their heads. *"FalalalaLAAAAAAAAAAAAAA!"*

It hit the dragon on the ear.

The startled dragon heaved. It gasped. It hiccupped. The fire rumbled in its chest and rolled up toward its throat. And out of its mouth, hundreds of tiny, shining lights exploded like a firecracker and whirled and whizzed and spiraled and swooped. And the cafeteria was like a night full of shooting stars—red and orange and yellow and green and blue and purple stars. As the children ran and leaped to catch them, the stars fell into their hands and turned into little paper snowflakes. Each one was different, and each one was beautiful.

But Henry just sat quietly, hugging his knees to his chest and feeling like a slowly rising soap bubble.

All the shapes inside him. All the shapes outside him. All the fearsome and wonderful shapes.

CHAPTER 17
OSCAR'S IDEA

PEOPLE ARE LIKE puzzle pieces. Put together, the shapes make a picture. And a friend is the one whose shape fits into your shape—fits perfectly because it is different, opposite, like a key in a lock, or a foot in a shoe.

As Henry watched his classmates dancing around the dragon, he realized that this puzzle was missing a piece. Oscar was gone.

Henry found him sitting in the little hallway, hunched over. Oscar was digging circles out of the napkins with a spoon and feeding them to his octagon. When Henry approached, he didn't even look up. And when he spoke, it wasn't about the dragon at all. "You never listen to my ideas," Oscar said.

That was not what Henry expected.

"It's always *Henry's a knight*, and *Henry's a superhero*, and *Henry's a cowboy*, and *Henry has a better idea*. You *never* listen to me."

Henry took off his helmet, which suddenly looked an awful lot like a plastic milk carton. He looked down and saw that several pieces of aluminum foil had fallen off his raincoat. There were bits of cheese stuck in his shoes. He didn't know what to say. He had made such a mess—with the dragon, and with Oscar.

"I want to be things too, you know," said Oscar.

Henry sat down. "I know."

"I mean, everyone's a knight now. So what's so special about being a knight?"

They could hear another ripple of laughter from the cafeteria. Oscar stuck out his lower lip and blew a puff of air that made the hair on his forehead fly up like the feathers of a bird. He scratched the Band-Aid on his elbow where he had fallen on the driveway last week while they were playing Batman and Robin. (Henry had been Batman.)

Henry rested his chin in his hands and stuck his nose into one sleeve of his armor. Inside of this sleeve he had written: **BE A LAWYER**. But he had scratched this out and written underneath: **BE LOYAL**, which, his dad had explained (much to his relief), did not mean wearing a suit and tie and going to court. It meant that your friend was your friend no matter what.

"Not everyone is a scientist," he said. "That takes a very specially-shaped brain."

Oscar wiped his nose on his sleeve. "That's true."

If I were going to draw a brand new Oscar, Henry thought, *I wouldn't change a single thing.*

"I'll be right back," Henry said, and when he returned, he was carrying his sketchbook. He laid it down on the floor beside Oscar and opened it up to a fresh page.

Make something new.

He drew the New Dragon, with its duck feet and its octopus arms and its butterfly wings and starbursts billowing around it. And then, on the dragon's shoulders, he drew Oscar—shining flying scientist Oscar, with shoelaces that twirled and trailed underneath him like a secret message written in clouds by an airplane, and with a shimmering mop of hair that danced in the wind. He drew Oscar's face—his pig face, his skunk face, his wonderful best friend face—and he even got the nose right. Oscar, the dinosaur tamer. Oscar, the hero. He was holding his octagon high above his head, so high it could nearly eat the moon, which was as big as a petri dish.

"Is that what I looked like on the *Stegosaurus*?" Oscar said in awe.

"No, you looked much better than this. I was kind of jealous."

"Of *me*?"

"Of you."

Oscar stared at the new picture for a long time. Then he nodded. "It's good."

The cafeteria door groaned. A little waterfall began pouring through the window hole and making a puddle by their shoes. Water was seeping again through the towels and the napkins and the washcloths and pooling on the floor.

"I'm sorry I laughed at your *Tyrannosaurus rex*," Oscar said.

"That's okay." Henry rubbed his chin and peered at his friend out of the corner of his eye. "Hey, we need to think of a way to get everyone out of the school since the slug slime glued us inside and the water keeps rising. I thought maybe we could gather all the spoons in the cafeteria and dig a tunnel to China."

Oscar looked at Henry. His eyes narrowed and his face stretched into a smile. "No. I have a better idea."

When they ran back into the cafeteria, all they could see was a whirlwind of peacock feathers spinning over the heads of a dancing circle of knights. "Come here!" called Henry. "We need you!" And to his astonishment and delight, the dragon who had been fleeing from his eraser all day long came immediately toward his outstretched arms and nuzzled its marshmallow-filled mouth under the hand of the boy who had drawn it—who had, instead of erasing it, given it a brand-new beautiful life.

Oscar climbed onto its scaly back and up its neck and stood between the trumpet and the kazoo on its head.

"Hand me my octagon!" Oscar said. The other kids lifted the bulging octagon up to him. It was nearly as big as Oscar now. "Now, let's fly! Fly to the ceiling!" And with a burst of notes from its trumpet-horn, the dragon lifted its colorful wings and rose. And lo and behold, there was Henry's picture, the picture he had just drawn for Oscar in the hallway, come alive before him: Oscar on top of the

New Dragon, holding his octagon high, being awesome.

Henry nudged Jade and whispered, "Sing," and she did:

> *All hail Sir Oscar! Hail his octagon!*
> *Come, fellow knights, and listen to my song!*
> *Into the beast's dark belly he did fall*
> *But no sour stench, no burp, no fireball*
> *Could hold him in that pit for long. Out! Out!*
> *He burst into the light again! Now shout*
> *His name from purple sea to purple sea:*
> *Oscar's plan will set La Muncha free!*

Reaching upward, Oscar drew a circle on the ceiling with a red marker. The octagon ate it. He drew a circle again, in the same spot, where the insulation was starting to poke out. The octagon eagerly chomped away. "See?" he cried. "The octagon can eat through all the *strata*! That means 'layers' in paleontologist language. I did an experiment in the kitchen so I knew it would work."

And he drew more and more circles, and the octagon grew larger and larger, and the dragon flew higher and higher, until with one final CRUNCH the roof gave way, and the sun came pouring through the hole. Oscar and the octagon, which had grown even larger than the dragon now, tumbled to the floor. And before anyone could stop it, the dragon jumped onto the octagon, bouncing on it like a big trampoline, and soared through the hole in the roof.

"Oscar," said Henry, gazing up at the circle of blue sky, "if this day were a chocolate-covered peanut, you would be the chocolate."

Oscar grinned. "And you would be the nut."

"I'm not a nut."

"Yes, you are. You're a *nutty* nut."

"You're a coconut."

"Macadamia nut."

"Walnut."

"Casheeewwwwwwww!" And they both bounced on the octagon and went flying through the hole after the dragon. One by one, the others followed them up onto the roof, and Mr. Bruce helped them climb down safely to the ground.

Then the cafeteria door burst, and the waters (and everything and everyone the waters were carrying) flooded into the cafeteria. And if Niagara Falls one day decided to get an education, it might look something like the soggy, sputtering fountain of people who came bouncing and climbing out of La Muncha Elementary School and spilling out onto the playground.

Once they were on dry ground, everyone was looking in the same direction: up. Above their heads, the dragon swooped and swirled and dove and wiggled in the wind.

"It's a duck!" said one teacher.

"It's a peacock!" said another.

"No, it's just a very large butterfly," said Mr. Boolean.

"It appears to be an airplane with very flexible arms—I mean, wings," said Mrs. Lightfoot.

And all the teachers—except Miss Pimpernel, who just smiled—began arguing over what kind of animal it was and whether it was a mallard or an American wigeon, or a monarch butterfly or a swallowtail, or a bird, or a reptile, and whether they should give their students a test about it tomorrow.

"It sort of looks like it met a Four," said Simon. "You know, what Miss Pimpernel said—when something is like something else?"

"You mean *metaphor*," said Jade.

"Hey, that sort of rhymes with dinosaur," said Oscar. "We can call it *Metaphorus rex*."

"You're a bonehead," Jade said, but the corners of her mouth were curling into a smile.

"Am not," said Oscar, trying not to smile back.

Principal Bunk was not happy. He had become unstuck from his chair at last, but his glued-on smile had come off with the rest of the slug slime. He tumbled onto the ground last of all, got to his feet, and smoothed his tie. Then, he too looked up.

And then he sat down on the pavement and cried.

"Mr.—" he sputtered through his tears, "Mr. Stompawog Laserfist!" For on the belly of the dragon, Henry had drawn a bright orange robot wearing boots and boxing gloves. But the rivers that glistened on the principal's cheeks were not rivers of sorrow, and his mouth began to form itself into that new shape that Henry had seen in his office—a shape that was his very own kind of happy.

The children, meanwhile, knew exactly what shape happiness was. Right there, right then, in that place, on that day, happiness was a quack-footed,

squishy-toothed,

purple-feathered,

peacock-eyed,

scribble-scrambled,

golden-horned,

zipper-singing,

wiggle-hugged

rainbow explosion of chalk and imagination.

And it smiled the most patched-up jumble of a dragon smile you've ever seen . . . a Thank-You smile and a That-Was-Delicious smile and a Look-How-Fabulous-I-Am smile and a You're-Not-So-Bad-Yourself smile and a What-Shall-We-Do-Today smile and an I-Like-Your-Socks smile all mixed together. The dragon sailed though the slippery wind and clambered up the clouds, until it finally disappeared from their sight.

"Jade," Henry said, as they stood staring up at the empty sky, "what do you want to be?"

Jade looked at him and scrunched her forehead into a little river of questions. "You mean when I grow up?"

Henry thought for a minute. "It doesn't seem like you should have to wait that long to *be* something."

"Okay, I want to be *unique.*"

Henry remembered Miss Brie saying that word when she was talking about his drawing. "You-what?"

"*Yoo-neek*. It means there's nothing else in the whole wide world like you."

Nothing else in the whole wide world. No one else who drew the way he drew.

"Do you want to wear my armor for a while?" It happened again! That was the trouble with talking—sometimes the words got away from you, like a dragon on the loose.

"*Really?*"

Henry gulped. He squirmed. He felt naked without his armor. He felt the opposite of invincible. But he unzipped it and held it out gently. Then he gasped.

All the chivalry was gone. The inside of the raincoat was completely blank—no words scribbled there at all—just like his bedroom door this morning!

Jade wrapped the armor around her and put the helmet proudly on her head, and no damsel had ever looked more knightly than she looked at that moment. Suddenly she bent down and touched her finger to the pavement. "Oh, there you are! I've been looking for you all day!" A little silvery worm-like thing crawled up her finger onto her palm and curled into a paperclip.

Then Henry knew what had happened to all his rules.

They had crawled right off his armor and through his skin. He felt like the Old Lady Who Swallowed a Spider, except instead of a spider it was his chivalry wriggling and giggling and tickling inside him. **DON'T FEED GIRLS TO DRAGONS** was tying itself around his stomach. And **LOOK BOTH WAYS BEFORE CROSSING THE STREET** was shimmying down his esophagus. And **SHARE YOUR THINGS** was swinging between his lungs. And **FIGHT FOR THE RIGHT** was burrowing a tunnel in his appendix. And **BE KIND** was squeezing under his ribcage. He was shivering and shimmering with chivalry. And when all the words had finally settled down into his guts, he could hear his heart tha-thump-tha-thumping, **BE BRAVE … BE BRAVE … BE BRAVE …**

Jade raised her paperclip high and yelled, "Sally forth!" And they all turned back toward the school.

Except there was no more school, because the octagon had eaten it. It was the yummiest, crunchiest circle of all.

CHAPTER 18
SIR HENRY'S QUEST

FEW SQUASHBUCKLERS BELIEVED that the Safest Elementary School in the County was done in by a mixed-up dragon and a hungry octagon. Theories bounced around about earthquakes and tornadoes and the environmental hazards of having too many bathrooms in one building. Scientists and weathermen and plumbers all came to study the ruins. The Bored Members came with their notebooks and shook their heads. But among the students, that day would always be remembered as the day that Henry Penwhistle's imagination escaped and ran wild.

There were many strange sightings in town—huge, colorful wings flapping outside windows, duck feet where

213

duck feet shouldn't be, an octopus sitting on telephone poles at night. More than one fair damsel dreamed of marshmallows and woke up in a bed full of fallen stars. A great composer who lived in Squashbuckle was inspired to write a duet for trumpet and kazoo that became famous all over the world. And an author far away heard it and wrote a book called *The Kazoo of the Dragon* that some people say is destined to be a classic.

Later, when a new school was built—square this time, not round—the dragon could sometimes be spotted outside the cafeteria window, eating the food that Miss Brie secretly threw out to it, while Mr. Bruce sat beside it on the curb, stroking its folded wings and telling it stories.

Oscar put his octagon on a strict diet until it fit back in the shoebox again.

Jade rescued a whole bus full of boys in distress.

And a week after their great adventure with the dragon, Oscar, Jade, and Henry leaned eagerly over the sofa in the Penwhistle house as Henry's parents sat with *Sir Henry's Quest* open on their laps and Furdinand licking their feet.

Henry watched page after page of his drawings flip past, like a movie of that bizarre, terrifying, wonderful day. He had worked all week on them, capturing in dizzy lines and squiggles of color everything he remembered of the octopus, the smiles of Miss Pimpernel, the chase through the school, the flooded hallway, the flight of the dinosaur, the battle with the Jabberwock, and the class's remaking of the dragon. Oscar had helped, reminding him of the details he forgot.

Jade, still glittering in the armor-raincoat, was finally reaching the end of a very long heroic song that she had composed especially for this occasion. Her words were like letters of gold dripping onto the pictures and making them a Book.

> *The World was all before them, where to choose*
> *Their next brave quest, and chivalry their guide:*
> *So side by side, with chalk and octagon,*
> *They sallied forth, galumphing on and on.*

She bowed. Furdinand howled. The Penwhistles burst into applause.

"What imaginations you all have!" cried Mr. Penwhistle. "To turn a little school plumbing emergency into a story like this!"

Henry, Oscar, and Jade glanced at each other. Henry's parents, of course, believed it was all a story the children had made up. But *they* knew better.

"That was an *awfully* scary dragon," Henry's mother said, as she had said before, standing in front of his bedroom door only a week ago.

"But if there's nothing scary, there's nothing to be brave about," said Henry. "And a knight must be brave."

"Well, you are *my* knight in shining armor. And Oscar!" Mrs. Penwhistle continued, turning to him. "That picture of you doing experiments in the kitchen . . . you looked like such a—such a scientist!"

Oscar's face was a glowing planet, ringed with a grin.

Mr. Penwhistle shook his head and winked at his son. "And here I thought you were up in your room playing with that silly Turbo-knuckle Nostril-crusher thing all week! But this—" He pounded a finger on the cover of the sketchbook. "This is the work of an *artist*, Squirt."

Henry flushed with both pride and embarrassment. "I'm not Squirt. I'm *Sir Henry*."

His father laughed. "I guess the name *Squirt* won't fit into an epic poem, will it? It doesn't rhyme with anything.

Except *blurt*. And *hurt*. And *shirt*. And—I know! *Skirt*."

"Dad. Knights do *not* wear a skirt."

"Sometimes they do!" said Jade, who was wearing a grass skirt her parents had bought in Hawaii. She wiggled, and the grass swished below the armor like the whispers of chivalry still wiggling inside of Henry, telling him all that he could be.

That night, after Oscar and Jade went home, Henry sat for a long time looking up at his bedroom door. He picked up a piece of chalk, but then put it down again. No. Not yet. For now, he liked it this way. Like a blank sheet of paper. Like a big rectangle of possibility. You have to be brave to be an artist, but you also have to be patient.

The door swung open as his mother came in. She walked to the window and drew the curtains wide, and the night stars gathered outside the glass, straining to see the knight and his adventures within. Mrs. Penwhistle sat beside Henry on the floor and stared up at the door with him.

"Aren't you going to draw anything, Henry?" she said. "You are so good at drawing."

"I'm waiting until I see it," he said.

"See what?"

"What I'm going to draw next." Henry was quiet for a
few moments. "There it is! A dancing zebra!"

"Where?"

"Don't you see its stripes spinning all around like a candy cane when you hold it between your hands and roll it back and forth? And its legs are kicking the stars away so it can go to sleep in the sky. *Look*."

His mother squinted at the empty black door. She turned her head one way and then the other. Henry heard a gentle rustling of wings. It was his mother's smile, flying past his new castle and Oscar's new laboratory and the overflowing chest of books, circling around the room, and finally coming to rest upon her face.

"I think I do, Henry," she said. The smile spread its wings across her cheeks. "I think I see it."

He picked up a new piece of chalk and began to draw.

THE END

KNIGHTS OF LA MUNCHA

BEING AN ARTIST (with chalk or music or words or anything else) can be lonely, discouraging, and scary. An artist should never have to stand alone. Thankfully, I've been surrounded by fellow knights who have aided both me and Sir Henry in our quest.

My agent Steven Malk was Henry's champion from the very first pages on, and I have deeply appreciated his support during this book's unpredictable journey.

Numerous people read drafts of the story and gave me critique and encouragement, including Gabrielle Rowe, Lanier Ivester, Sarah Clarkson, Rebecca Reynolds, Tracy Mack, Jonathan Rogers, Kami Rice, Laure Hittle, the

Brewer family, the Carlson family, and the Aman family.

Heroic illustrator Benjamin Schipper brought Henry's imagination to life with his magic pencil and with admirable chivalry.

Barbara Fisch and Sarah Shealy kindly and expertly sallied forth alongside us to help the book find its readers.

The Rabbit Room community (I promise Henry's anti-bunny ire is not meant for you), both in my Nashville neighborhood and beyond, has flooded me with love and support for the past six years, believing in me even when I, like Henry, doubted myself. Every artist should be so lucky to have as loyal an army of knights beside her.

My ever-growing family—both on the Trafton side and the Peterson side—is my constant source of laughter and inspiration and comfort, the paper wrapper soaring off the end of my drinking straw. To my parents: thank you, thank you for giving my wild imagination space to run free, grow, and flourish.

The former Jones Jaggers Elementary School in Bowling Green, Kentucky, (where I attended from first through seventh grade) unwittingly loaned its circular building shape to Henry's school—but that is where the similarity ends.

I'm deeply indebted to its wise principal and its superhero teachers, who read aloud great stories that inspired me (including many that found their way into Henry's book chest) and who encouraged my creativity.

Finally, there's no one (including me), I think, who loves Henry's story as fiercely as my husband Pete does. He is my best friend, my bard, my circus strongman, and the seeker of my smiles. For a great many reasons, this book might never have found its way into the world without him.

To all of the above:

I dub thee **KNIGHTS OF LA MUNCHA**.

And to you, readers: The quest is real. Art is powerful. Will you join us? What new and beautiful things will you make, brave knights?

HENRY'S BOOK CHEST

HENRY'S STORY REFERS to many classic books and poems. Here are some you might enjoy reading:

The *Adventures of Pinocchio* by CARLO COLLODI

Alice in Wonderland and *Through the Looking Glass*
 (which includes "Jabberwocky") by LEWIS CARROLL

Bunnicula by DEBORAH HOWE and JAMES HOWE

Charlie and the Chocolate Factory by ROALD DAHL

The Chronicles of Narnia by C. S. LEWIS

Harold and the Purple Crayon by CROCKETT JOHNSON

"The Jumblies" by EDWARD LEAR

King Arthur and His Knights of the Round Table by ROGER LANCELYN GREEN

"The Legend of Sleepy Hollow" by WASHINGTON IRVING

The Mouse and the Motorcycle by BEVERLY CLEARY

Peter Pan by J. M. BARRIE

Treasure Island by ROBERT LOUIS STEVENSON

Where the Wild Things Are by MAURICE SENDAK

Winnie-the-Pooh by A. A. MILNE

The Wizard of Oz by L. FRANK BAUM

ABOUT THE AUTHOR

JENNIFER TRAFTON is the author of *The Rise and Fall of Mount Majestic*, which was a nominee for Tennessee's Volunteer State Book Award and the National Homeschool Book award. *Henry and the Chalk Dragon* (a runner-up for *World Magazine's* 2017 Children's Novel of the Year) arose from her lifelong love of art and her personal quest for the courage to be an artist. When she's not writing or drawing, she teaches creative classes and workshops in a variety of schools, libraries, and homeschool groups, as well as online classes to kids around the world. She lives in Nashville, Tennessee, along with her husband, an energetic border collie, and a long-suffering chicken.

WWW.JENNIFERTRAFTON.COM

ABOUT THE ILLUSTRATOR

BENJAMIN SCHIPPER is also the illustrator of *The Most Frightening Story Ever Told* by Phillip Kerr (Knopf, 2016). He lives with his wife in Greenville, South Carolina, where in addition to working on his own projects he teaches art at a homeschool co-op.

WWW.BENJAMINSCHIPPER.COM

Also by

Jennifer Trafton

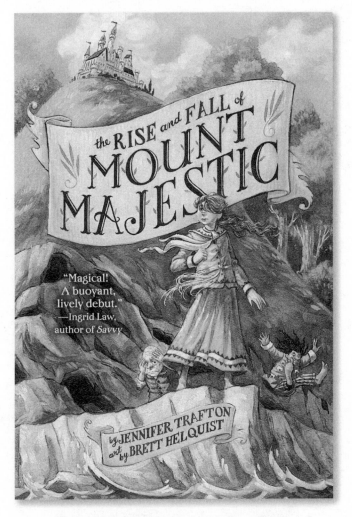

Dial Books for Young Readers, 2010

RABBIT ROOM
— PRESS —
Nashville, Tennessee

www.RABBITROOM.com